golfoholics™
THE FRONT NINE

GOLF STORIES BY
CHASE BALATA

For information about permission to reproduce or transmit
selections from this book in any form or by any means, write to:

Permissions, Hot House Press, 760 Cushing Highway,
Cohasset, MA 02025

This is a work of fiction. Names, characters, places and inci-
dents are either the product of the author's imagination or are
used fictitiously.

Library of Congress Cataloging-in-Publication Data

Balata, Chase, 1955-
  Golfoholics : the front nine golf stories / by Chase Balata.
    p. cm.
  ISBN 0-9755245-3-4
1. Golf stories, American. I. Title.
PS3602.A594G65 2006
813'.6--dc22

                                    2006002475

    Printed in the United States of America

Book design by Rebecca Krzyzaniak
Front cover design Sparky's Garage
Illustrations by John C. Lund

Hot House Press
760 Cushing Highway
Cohasset, MA 02025
www.hothousepress.com

To Dad
Without you, this book would be
just another pipe dream.
You the (old) man.
The next round's on me.

Love and Couples,
Chase

The author gratefully acknowledges:

His wife for turning him onto the game. His kids for having the good sense to take up tennis. John Pfeifer and the grease monkeys at Sparky's Garage for the logo. Rand Kramer and the crew at Siteworx for the website. Jon C. Lund for the illustration. Phil Palmeri for the inspiration.

May the course be with you.

golfoholics™
THE FRONT NINE

A.K.A. A.K.A.

Francis X. Sullivan was a nickname magnet. He was Frank. Frankie. Franko.

FX. X-Man. XS. Effin XS. Effin.

Sully. Van. Vandaman. Van Gogh. VG. Sully Van Gogh.

In fact, he had so many names, he was also known as A.K.A.

But he might as well have been called Teflon, because none of these names stuck until Skully came along. And when that moniker reared its boney head, it stuck like a high wedge shot landing on a soft wet green.

Its tenacious origins can be traced to the day Frank and his golf buddy Chester Banes were teamed up in a Member-Member at the River Creek Club. It was a two-man team best ball tournament that found them 7 under after sixteen holes. They were on fire. But then something happened that took them out of the zone and into the *Twilight Zone*.

Frankie had birdied the previous hole and had honors on the 17th, a 195-yard par three along the Potomac River. The pin was tucked in the back left portion of the green, a peninsula protected by a massive waste bunker that wrapped around the front and left side. The hole was probably playing closer to 205 that day and the air was dead still and heavy with late spring Virginia humidity.

"Whaddya think?" Banes asked his partner. "Easy 5-wood?"

"Too much," Franko said decisively, pulling the

4-iron from his bag.

"You may want a little schwing lube in that case." Chester offered his partner an old beat-up pewter flask filled with single malt. "Allow me to introduce you to my good friend Glen."

"Ah, Dr. Livet I presume," FX replied, reaching for the flask. "So nice to make your acquaintance." As he took a swig of the Glenlivet, a pair of Canada geese flew in from the river and settled on the white tee box for a front row seat.

"Are we gonna play golf one of these days?" asked Fred, one of their opposing twosome.

"Or would you guys rather have a freakin' tee party?" his partner Al chimed in.

"Hey, do I interrupt your pre-shot routine?" X-Man asked, putting his ball on a tee.

"Grip it and rip it Sull," urged Banes.

With that, Sully stood over his ball and emptied his mind, savoring the warmth of the single malt emanating from his gut. He eyed his target envisioning the ball flight, a subtle draw starting at the center of the green and arcing magnetically toward the pin. He took a full backswing and then some, determined not to leave the ball short and in the beach.

His hips began to pivot.

His arms found the slot.

As the club head neared maximum velocity, one of the geese issued a premature "You da man" that came out as a loud "HONK HONK HONK."

The interruption shattered Van Gogh's artful concentration causing him to lift his head ever so slightly which in turn lifted the club head an inch too high, resulting in a low screaming zonker.

But the ball wasn't the only thing that was skulled. On the white tee box, the head of one of the geese exploded in a sickening SPLAT! Sending feathers, blood and guts in all directions. The headless goose did the Texas two-step on the tee box as if looking for its noggin while its partner looked on in horror. "HONK?"

The foursome back at the blue tees was speechless until Chester broke the silence.

"I'd say you skulled that one, Skully." It was inadvertent. It was brilliant. It was adhesive.

"Skully. . . . That's perfect!" chuckled Fred.

"Skully," Al tried it on for size. "Skully, Skully, Skully," he repeated, liking the fit.

The headless goose collapsed and died.

Skully let out a belated "FORE!" and stood on the tee with the 4-iron propping him up, shaking his head. The living goose came around from the shock of seeing its mate beheaded and began honking angrily.

Next thing you know it was running toward Skully, honking away, wings flapping, taking dead aim at him and taking to the air like a guided missile.

Skully just stood there staring at the dead goose.

"SKULLY!" Banes yelled.

"HONK!" the angry goose cried.

Skully bowed his head in shame, or prayer, or maybe just resignation as the goose opened its beak and excavated a patch of scalp, leaving a gaping bloody V-shaped chevron that would follow Skully around for the rest of his life. And taking a prized possession in the process—his '86 Masters hat. Signed by Nicklaus.

"MY HAT!" Skully screamed in vain as the goose ascended over the Potomac, as good as in Canada. "COME BACK HERE WITH MY LUCKY HAT!" Skully shook his fist at the migrating bird.

"An eye for an eye," Fred observed.

"A hat for a head." Ray concluded. "Banes, you're up."

"You know what they say," Banes added, teeing it up. "What goose around, comes around."

Collective moans filled the air as Banes teed off, skying a 5-wood into the bunker.

The boys finished up the last two holes double/double dropping to 3 under and out of the running for any prize money. They returned to the scene of the crime after the round to bury the headless goose, but she was nowhere to be found.

"Must have wandered off," Banes suggested.

Skully fashioned a cross out of a long tee and a shorter one and inserted it into the riverbank off 17. Banes hummed "Oh Canada."

"I suppose I should say a prayer," Skully admitted. "Let's see, friends may come and friends may go."

Banes cut in, "And friends may peter out you know."

And together, arms around each other's shoulders, they extolled "But we'll be friends through thick and thin. Peter out, or peter in."

The sun set casting an orange glow on the Potomac while Skully and Banes drank a toast to the goose, the Masters cap, and last, but not least, Skully's new name.

"I feel terrible about the goose," Skully confessed.

"Not your best shot," Banes admitted. "Although it did give new meaning to the term "birdie." How's your head?"

"A little crusty," Skully replied reaching back to inspect the damage. "But I've seen worse."

"I'm sure you have," Banes agreed, contemplating Skully's previous life as a Navy SEAL.

Skully smirked and offered his friend a cigar. Banes accepted and reciprocated by proffering Glen once again. They sat there on the bank of the river smoking and sipping. Like the river, they were calm on the surface with a strong current running below them.

Until Banes' cell phone rang.

"Banes," he answered.

"Fred," said the phone. "C'mon up to the club, we're all having dinner. And make sure you bring Skully."

Banes hung up and turned to Skully. "That was Sir Frederick. Our presence is requested in the dining room."

The two of them ascended the hill to the clubhouse. The post-tournament celebration was in high gear on the back patio. And they all seemed to be gathered around an oversized grill that Skully and Banes recognized as belonging to Fred.

"Fred, since when does the club cook on your grill?" Skully asked his neighbor.

"When we're cooking your goose!" he said maniacally and flung open the top of the barbecue.

There lay the headless goose on the grill. "Take a gander at that!" Fred said, cutting a wedge from its breast and holding out the fork to Skully. "See if she's cooked to your liking."

As Skully bit into the bird and the crowd shook with laughter, Banes appeared with a couple of Harps and handed one to the golfer formerly known as Frank, Hank, Shank, Shank Williams, XS, and Sully.

"I christen thee Skully," Banes said, pouring an ounce of beer on his friend's chewed up head.

"TO SKULLY," cheered the crowd, clanking their glasses together. Skully took a long pull off the Harp and returned the toast:

"With friends like these…who needs enemas?"

And with those appetizing words, they sat down to dinner.

BLUE MOON

As Friday evening drew to a close, Banes slipped out of his house near midnight under a full moon to rendezvous with Skully for their first Blue Moon Midnight Madness Match, a late-night lunar-lighted eighteen-hole two-man immersion into the all-too-familiar land of temporary insanity.

Skully's latest girlfriend Barb, a drop-dead gorgeous astronomer from NASA, planted the seed earlier in the evening as Banes and his wife Gwen were dining with them in Skully's sunroom. As Stargirl regaled them with facts about the stratosphere, she happened to point out the window and mention that this was the last blue moon they'd see until the end of June, 2007 when there would next be two full moons in the same month.

Skully and Banes, being wired similarly, wasted no time hatching the night's festivities. They looked across the table at each other in the blue moonlight. Skully mouthed the word "18." Banes replied with a silent "Midnight."

"Huh?" Skully mouthed, not understanding.

"Midnight." Banes mouthed again, raising one finger then two.

"Buckle my shoe?" Skully mouthed.

"NO. MIDNIGHT. 1-2. 12," Banes mouthed in a loud whisper.

"What about midnight?" Gwen wanted to know.

"Oh, I was just singing to myself dear," Banes lied. "*After midnight…*"

"*We gonna let it all hang out,*" Skully joined in, and the two former high school bandmates sere-

12

naded the women with a J.J. Cale tune.

"Boys will be noise," Gwen said to Barb while shaking her head.

After dinner, the boys managed to dig up an appropriate trophy from Skully's library that the winner would display until the next blue moon. It was an old blue metal lunar globe.

So a few hours later, comfortably numb from the anesthesia Skully had been serving all evening, Banes slinked across his backyard in the brisk November air to the blue tees on number 7 at River Creek, a magnificent and secluded spot on the bank of Goose Creek that his home sat above.

"What took you?" asked Skully emerging from the shadows, a smoldering Fuente dangling from his lips.

"Had to wait till Gwen fell asleep," Banes replied. "She already thinks my infatuation with this game is a bit over the top. Imagine me telling her I'm going out in the middle of the night to play a round under a full moon. I may be thinking green jacket, but she'd be thinking straight jacket."

"Justifiably so," observed Skully with a raised eyebrow.

"Where's Barbarella?" Banes wondered. "I figured she'd be our caddy for the event."

"She's running a half-marathon in the morning so I put her to bed."

As if on cue, they heard a knocking coming from Skully's bedroom window overlooking the battleground. As they glanced up, they saw Barb turn her back to them, lift her robe and press her cheeks against the glass, surely the loveliest moon in the sky that night.

"That's quite a sendoff. What does she do for an encore?"

"'Fraid that was the encore. I got the sendoff before coming out here," Skully winked as he swaggered up to the tee. "What kind of ball you playing?"

Banes reached in his pocket and pulled out a couple of Titleists. "ProV1."

"I borrowed a few of the Club's Pinnacle practice balls for the occasion," Skully said. "Figured when I lose them in the dark, I won't be as pissed off."

"Good luck."

"Same. We'll need it in this light."

Skully abstained from a practice swing and addressed his ball. "Mully on the first?"

"If you must."

The 7th green was bathed in steely blue moonlight giving it an eerie glow below them. The pin was tucked up on the upper tier in its best sucker position. Gunning it at the hole risks being wet with a miss to the right, or a sandy if it's long and left. The smart play, particularly at this hour, is to aim for the heart of the green and hope for a couple of good putts.

Skully hit a high 8-iron from 162 out and a light breeze threatened to carry it to the upper tier, but his ball didn't make the crest of the slope and rolled back down to the center of the green.

"Nice shot," Banes complimented him, knowing his play now was to go for the gusto, lending further veracity to the old saying "A sucker is born every minute."

He teed up his ProV1 and closed his eyes envisioning the perfect swing.

The hole-in-one-big-beautiful-starlit-arching-puréed-dead-on-pin-seeking-cup-filling-ass-kicking-swing-of-a-7-iron. The wambamthankyoumam queen of golf shots.

He imagined snuggling up to the hole with her, banging against the pin while the flag waved above in celebration. A catharsis that had always managed to elude him. But the dream lingered on.

"At this rate, we won't get 9 in before dawn," Skully needled.

Banes awoke from his reverie and summoned up a languid swing sending the ball skyward where a dark cloud picked a fine time to obscure the moon and dim the lights.

"Felt good," he mumbled, hoping for the best.

"'Fraid I lost it, Banes," Skully confessed. "Hit a provisional."

Chester took his advice and reloaded.

Once again, he hit what he thought was a good shot, but the moonlight proved to be an elusive source of illumination.

"Whose idea was this anyway?" Banes wondered aloud.

"Our eyes will adjust to it eventually," his friend reassured him with the kindly optimism befitting a guy who's pretty sure he's just bagged the first skin.

"Lots of golf to be played."

Which wasn't exactly the truth.

They walked down over the bridge to the green and Skully bent over to fix his ball mark. "Another foot and mine was tight," he remarked, reveling in the land of what might have been.

"Yeah, and if your aunt had a dick she'd be your uncle," Banes reminded him.

"If I were you, I'd worry less about my aunt's dick and more about your balls," Skully one-upped.

Banes scoured the green but didn't see a thing. Then he noticed a ball peeking out from under a layer of sand in one of the back traps. "Here it is."

"That your first or second?"

"No way of knowing. They're both Titleist 1s." They searched for another minute or two for his other ball to no avail.

"Probably in the creek," Banes admitted before descending into the bunker. He got his footing, opened up the face of his sand wedge and gave it his best Azinger. It was a good out, as the ball landed four or five feet to the left of the pin. But it was loaded with spin, which pulled the Titleist tauntingly close to the cup before gravity sucked it down the hill leaving him thirty feet from the hole.

"YSA buddy," Skully declared with a smirk before breaking into a low-volume bastardization of "YMCA." "YSA, you're still away."

"It's a bit early for celebration isn't it Skull?" Banes gave the trap a cursory rake and headed to his ball.

"Go on and putt. You can show me the line," Skully said as he walked up the slope to tend the pin. Banes put a good stroke on the ball and up the hill it went over the crest and toward the cup.

As it approached, Skully yanked the pin and out of the cup popped an unexpected surprise: Banes' missing ball.

"Holy shite," Skully changed his tune.

"NO!" Banes shook his head in disbelief. "It's not a ProV1, is it?"

Skully picked up the culprit and eyed it carefully. "I don't believe it."

Banes' heart reverberated loud enough to wake the neighbors. "But...but...which is my first ball?"

A mad laugh began to emanate from somewhere deep inside Skully, acknowledging his friend's dilemma. It only took a moment before Banes joined him, and but another before the two of them were howling at the moon and rolling on the green.

They laughed until their guts ached, and howled until lights appeared in one of the homes bordering the hole. A pissed off neighbor appeared on his deck and shouted, "What the hell's going on down there? Skully, Banes, is that you?"

Skully broke free of the lunacy just long enough to tell him of their predicament. "Yeah, it's us, Fred. Banes here just aced the hole. Only…ah ha ha ha."

"Only I hit a Mully," Banes added. "And I don't know which ball went in the ho-ho-hole."

"Only one thing to do," Fred said with authority.

"What's that?" Banes wondered, in desperate need of a cure for the madness that had him in its grasp.

"Open up your bar, Banesy ol' boy. Drinks are on you. I'll alert the troops."

Skully and Banes looked wide-eyed at each other overtaken by the realization that this was indeed what must happen.

"Drinks on Banes," Skully shouts to Fred and the moon, both of whom look back at him in amusement.

Moments later, they're in Chester's basement cracking a beer as Fred and a half-dozen other golf buddies from the neighborhood appeared to offer both their congratulations and commiseration. Skully recounted the story, and asked the question of the hour, "Was it a legit hole-in-one, or a Mulligan hole-in-one?"

Banes just shook his head as his friend continued, "Only his hairdresser knows for sure."

The guys shared a good laugh over Chester's predicament, and after another round, someone dug up an old Frank Sinatra record and the gang started serenading Banes at the top of their lungs with "Blue Moon."

Suddenly a woman's voice cut through the hoopla. "WHAT'S GOING ON HERE?"

Gwen appeared on the stairs, and quiet engulfed the room until Fred broke the silence.

"Gwen, your husband just shot a hole in one."

"HUH? AT THIS HOUR?"

"Let's say he may have," Skully qualified the statement and proceeded to tell her the story.

"Well, isn't anyone going to offer me a beer?" Gwen wondered. "I've been waiting twenty years for this day. Or night, rather."

That only sent the room up for grabs, and someone passed Gwen a cold one. She raised her bottle to her husband in a toast as the clock struck one.

"Here's to you, Ace."

Did I or didn't I? Banes wondered staring out the window at three am. Outside, the blue moon grinned above the 7th green reminding Banes that the uncertainty will drive him loony.

He awoke the next morning, groggy and strangely elated, a feeling that grew when he opened his front door and found the lunar globe on his stoop. Taped to its base was a note in Skully's best scrawl: Rematch under the next full moon.

Banes walked back into the house, displayed the trophy on his mantle, cranked up the Sinatra CD that was still in the stereo, and serenaded the globe with an off-key "Blue Moon."

THE INSIDE TRACK

It was a dark and stormy night. Followed by a dark and stormy day. Followed by another dark and stormy night and day.

Rinse. And repeat.

There would be no spring fever for Skully and Banes this year. Only cabin fever. A steady diet of the Golf Channel interspersed with washing clubs and polishing balls. With the occasional rerun of *The Dick Van Dyke Show* thrown in to break up the monotony.

Gwen noticed their plight and decided to help out by sending her husband to the supermarket.

Anything to get him and that golfoholic friend of his out of the house.

She gave Banes a shopping list so they wouldn't get lost in the beer aisle. Among other sundry items, the boys were to dig up eggs, Italian bread and paper cups. A recipe for disaster if ever there was one.

Banes was inspecting a dozen eggs when Skully approached with a baguette slung over his shoulder like he was *The Rifleman*. He grabbed one of the eggs from the carton and placed it on the floor. Banes was on to him, and opened the sleeve of cups, placing one fifteen feet away.

Skully took the baguette out of its bag and lined up his shot. Standing over the egg, he gently putted it toward the cup. The egg wobbled and wound up way short.

"Dropped your lipstick," Banes needled.

"Skirt blew up in my face," Skully took it in

stride. "You know, though, this gives me an idea. Since it's too wet to play outdoors, why don't we tee it up inside?" Skully was a fountain of wonderfully awful ideas such as this.

"Inside?" Banes asked, taking the semolina from him.

"The great indoors. We'll set up courses in our houses."

"Try your house. Gwen would have my ass."

"My house then," Skully agreed.

"You're on." Banes drew back the sesame semolina declaring "*I am the egg man*" before whacking the balata wannabe so hard that the shell shattered and raw egg flew every which way, particularly Skully's way. "*Coo coo cachew.*"

"That's a fine way to treat the host of the new Inside Open." He retaliated by winging one at Banes. Before you know it, they'd grabbed a dozen apiece and were hiding behind end-cap displays

lobbing yolky grenades down the aisle at each
other.

Skully was left holding the last egg, and he knew
he had the upper hand. But Banes diffused the situation by swinging the semolina like a bat and throwing the gauntlet. "You a pitcha, or a glass of wawa?"

Skully pulled down his cap and coiled in his
wind-up. After nodding off a couple of signals from
his imaginary catcher, he winged the egg by Banes
who swung and whiffed. It landed with a splat in
the cart of a woman in the express checkout line,
too absorbed in *The National Enquirer* to even
notice. The groceries beside her were covered in
raw scrambled egg.

"Boy, did you get away with murder there,"
Banes said shaking his head at the pitcher.

"So far," Skully admitted. "But wait'll she reaches
for something in her cart. I'm gonna have a hard
time keeping a straight face."

"We better head her off at the pass." Banes put one foot on the shopping cart and with the other pedaled the big scooter down the soft-drink aisle toward express checkout. On the way, he reached out and grabbed a six-pack of ginger beer.

"What's that for?" Skully asked sprinting alongside him.

"Dark and Stormies. The antidote to this weather."

"Ah, Bermuda rum and ginger beer. The official beverage of the Inside Open. I'll get the limes," Skully offered and dashed into produce.

Banes underestimated the amount of time required to bring a speeding shopping cart to a full stop and ended up using the spacious derriere of the woman absorbed in *The Enquirer* as a backstop.

"My word! I have never…" she stammered turning around with a scowl.

"I'm so sorry. You see, one of my patients has just

29

gone into labor," Banes apologized and improvised. "Would you mind terribly if I went before you?"

The woman's expression changed. "Oh, not at all, doctor. At what hospital are you delivering?" She positively beamed at him now.

Banes steered the cart around hers and began emptying its contents on the tarmac. "Reston," he lied.

"Oh, my sister's a neo-natal nurse there, you must know her—Brenda Stemplekoski?

"Ah, Brenda, wonderful woman," Banes nodded, ran his credit card through the check out machine and stared impatiently at the LED readout hungry for a conclusion to the transaction. The lie squeezed him in its tenacious grasp.

Skully appeared, limes in hand, a welcome distraction. "Playing through!" he bellowed and tossed the citrus onto the conveyor belt. "Excuse us, we'll be late for our tee time!"

Banes' gut sank. He signed the credit card slip and looked at Skully shaking his head. "Now doctor, you know we have to see to that C-section over at Reston Hospital first." Then looking at the woman, he confides in her, "My colleague here is the anesthesiologist and I fear he's been partaking, if you know what I mean."

"Gave myself an epidural in the produce section," Dr. Skully added. The woman gave him a quizzical look.

As they made their exit, she yelled after Banes, "Doctor, what's your name? I'll tell Brenda you said hi."

"Kildare," he yelled back.

The woman was digesting this as she reached into her cart.

"And I'm Mrs. Kildare," Skully added flitting out the door.

As her hand made contact with the raw egg she

let out a soft scream. By then the boys were running for the car. They hightailed it over to Home Depot for a couple of pieces of Astroturf for a makeshift tee and green. On the way, Skully broke into an old Stones' tune.

"Oh doctor, please help me, I'm damaged."

"There's a pain, where there once was a heart," Banes crooned back at him.

Thankfully, it was a short drive, and their eardrums were spared too much abuse. Astroturf in hand, they proceeded to Leesburg Golf for some Wiffle golf balls. And the local ABC store for a bottle of Goslings Black Seal Rum.

"'Cause I'm down in Virginia, with your cousin Luke," Skully picked up where they left off in his best Jagger falsetto.

"And there'll be no wedding today," Banes answered.

"So doctor, please help us, we're damaged," they sang together.

By the time they reached Banes' driveway, Skully had the rum open and a shot poured into the bottle cap. "Anesthesiologist's orders," he offered Banes the cap.

"Shank you doctor," he accepted. Skully followed suit. "To your health, Doc."

As they walked into the house, Gwen took one look at them, rain and egg drenched, and shook her head. "I smell trouble."

"I showered this morning," her husband replied planting the groceries on the counter and a kiss on her cheek. "Even used deodorant."

"And rum for mouthwash?" Gwen noticed.

"A little Goslings, is all," he confirms. "Gotta run, Hun, late for our tee time."

"In this weather?"

"We're playing indoors. At Skully's, of course," he adds.

"But of course," Gwen raises an eyebrow at her

33

husband. "You two are golfopaths. I swear, it's like a disease."

"We better leave, Honey, it may be contagious." Skully and Banes left the house via the garage so Banes could grab his clubs. They walked next door through the rain to Skully's place and went right to the kitchen to mix up a little rum, ginger beer and lime.

"Let it rain," Banes toasted.

"To victory at sea," Skully raised his glass. In the distance, thunder rumbled like artillery.

They descended to Skully's basement to cut a hole in the Astroturf and sculpt a green. Banes drew a palette-like design on back of the turf and Skully took a blade to it. When he cut the hole out, Banes picked it up and proclaimed "Our trophy."

"The Official Dark and Stormy Hole," Skully named it.

"It makes a nice coaster," Banes observed, placing his drink on it.

"Or yarmulke," said Skully retrieving it and placing it on his head.

"Oys will be oys," Banes noted.

"All right, we better get this round started while there's still some daylight left," Skully suggested, getting down to business. "Let's see who goes first," he motioned, flipping a tee in the air. It landed in Banes' drink.

"That would be me." Banes took the tee and skewered his lime with it. "Do I get to place the green?" he asked his opponent.

"So be it," Skully answered. "After that, whoever wins the hole places it."

"That's whomever," his linguistic friend corrected him while walking upstairs and tucking the green in Skully's fireplace.

"Whatever. Dollar skins?"

"Make it two," Banes insisted, placing the tee box in the kitchen. "The 1st hole is a 425-inch par four. Quiet please."

No cameras flashed as he teed off with a 7-iron and the inaugural round of the Inside Open commenced. The ball landed on the couch in front of the fireplace.

"Nice drive," Skully said, adding, "but a difficult lie." He took an 8-iron sending his Wiffle Ball over the kitchen counter cutting off the dogleg to the green. It ricocheted off a lampshade before coming to rest on the rug a mere yard from the green. "Yes!" he exclaimed.

"That was a member's bounce if ever I saw one," Banes complained.

"Home course advantage," Skully claimed.

Banes took off his shoes and climbed up on the couch wielding a wedge. Precariously balanced with one foot on the arm, he chopped down at the ball which was wedged between two cushions. It came out hot and knocked a framed photo of Skully and his ex-wife off the mantle that fell to the floor with a crash. A crack appeared in the glass running between the former couple.

"Whoops," Banes mumbled and stooped to pick it up.

"Leave it," Skully commanded. "Don't know why it was still up there anyway." Taking a sand wedge, he chipped his ball into the fireplace where it came to rest on the green.

"You're dancing," Banes congratulated him. "On in regulation. But I have faith that you can 3-putt from there."

Skully won the first and the ice was broken. The next hole was a long par five going upstairs and into a bathroom where Skully placed the green in a tub filled with a half inch of water. He fell prey to his own cleverness though, and found himself taking two shots to get out of the water hazard once he got up there.

The boys played through bedrooms and bathrooms, living room and dining room, library and rec room where Skully took a divot out of his pool table. "My winnings will pay to fix it," he declared, up seven skins going into the last hole.

"In that case, I press," Banes challenged.

"I accept," Skully said, placing the 18th green in the kitchen sink.

They teed off in the front hall nearly taking a valuable painting off the wall with Skully's errant duck hook of a drive.

The ball trickled into a closet.

"Doors open," Banes observed, before driving a 4-iron down the narrow fairway. After Skully chipped out of the closet, Banes lobbed a sand wedge into a half-full wine glass by the sink. Skully found the green on his next shot.

"Pressure's on, Banes old boy."

Banes got up on the kitchen counter and looked down at his ball swimming in last night's Cabernet. "Do I get relief?"

"Keep dreaming. Play it as it lies."

Taking his putter, Banes gently took it back and followed through sending the glass shattering to the counter and ejecting its payload into the sink and down the hole. Red wine redecorated the kitchen.

From the stereo, Mick Jagger sang *"Shattered"* on cue. Banes pranced on the counter, singing harmonies into his putter. *"I'm in tatters."*

Skully cranked the volume and poured a couple more Dark and Stormies.

Jagger sang, *"My brain's been splattered. All over Manhattan."*

"Shit, shitdoobie, shattered," Banes bellowed pulling a ten spot from his pocket to settle the bet

and handing it to Skully who in turn handed his friend a drink.

Outside the rain swelled Goose Creek and the 7th green looked more like a water hazard than a putting surface.

"To the Inside Open," Banes toasted.

"Another round?" Skully inquired.

"Is zee Pope Catholic?" Banes replied, placing the Astroturf trophy on his head and his ball on the first tee.

RORE MUM!

"You live for this tournament, don't you?" Gwen asked with an undercurrent that intimated of misbegotten priorities, misspent youth and miss-whomeveritisyouseewhileyouescapetoyourold-stompingground.

"Whaddya mean?" Banes replied with articulation befitting the circumstances. He knew that she was referring to the annual Devereux-Emmet Invitational he played in every year at the GC Golf Club.

Banes' wife just glared at him and declared, "You know damn well what I mean." He gave her a wink, grabbed his golf bag and made for the door when she added, "Just make sure you bring home the crystal this year."

Ah, the crystal. The prize coveted by the wives of all the Neanderthals who played in this tournament. Banes and his buddy Dick who invited him to the Member-Guest had gotten their hands on it year one, a Waterford salad bowl bearing the club's attractive thistle logo. But this was the 7th annual DEI, so they were due to once again return home bearing some booty. Or they sure as hell wouldn't be getting any.

Banes had known Richard Pritcher, or Dick Yaprickya, as he'd always called him, since he could tie his shoelaces. Dick had been a legend around the golf club ever since the ballwasher incident, an unfortunate event that occurred at the tournament a few years ago. It happened shortly after he and Banes had teed off on number 7, when they heard some guys bellow out from an adjoining fairway. Turned out it was a couple of their high school buddies, Cavanaugh and Hedge, who were also playing in the Member-Guest. While most players walked with caddies, Banes and Yaprickya, due to their proficiency at the game, were in the Z-flight and were relegated to riding due to a shortage of bag sherpas. They were about to drive off in their cart when the guys called their names and they turned and hurled a few expletives back at them.

Problem was, Dick had his foot on the gas and proceeded to run over the ballwasher, shearing it from its mooring. Next thing you know, the cart was stuck on top of the severed hunk of iron, and they weren't going anywhere. Banes got out and tried to lift it off while Yaprickya gunned it, but all Banes got was a face full of mud.

By this time, Cavanaugh and Hedge were rolling on the fairway. That evening over cocktails on the back porch, the club president presented Dick with a driver's license application while the crowd broke out in a chorus of *"I'm a Ballwasher"* to the tune of "Girlwatcher," a catchy little tune they sang repeatedly that evening.

But there would be no ballwasher fiascos this year. Banes and Yaprickya were here to win, dammit. Baby needs new Waterford. And while there was no guarantee this year will be any different than the last five, they were always assured of at least bringing home the annual gift to the players. Last year it was a coffee table book detailing the history of the club. This year, it was a small black leatherette suitcase on wheels. With any luck, Banes would be wheeling home the crystal in it.

Friday was a breathtaking day, particularly if you were walking the course with a stogie hanging from your lips. They would play three nine-hole matches today, followed by two the next. They'd be done by Saturday afternoon, and still have time to spend half the weekend with their wives, if they weren't busy checking into the Betty Ford Clinic or the fat farm.

At breakfast they were treated to sausage, bacon, eggs, rolls and butter. Lunch was a light repast of burgers, brats and dogs. Then dinner found them shoving a boatload of fried shrimp and cherry-stones into their pie holes, followed by brisket, tar tar, sauerbraten and 24-ounce steaks that were four inches thick. Dessert was an angioplasty.

And in between all the food was the incessant flow of beer, scotch or whatever lit their fire. For Dick Yaprickya, it was rum. Knowing that, Banes had a bottle of Mount Gay stashed in his bag that they began to delve into by the 2nd hole of the first match. Their opponents were both unnerved and horrified that they were hitting the bottle so hard so early. But for Banes and Yaprickya, there was always a lot of catching up to do, as it was the only time the wives permitted them to get together all year.

By the 4th hole, Dick was in the woods whacking at his ball, but it ricocheted off two trees and flew out of bounds. He meant to say "More rum" but instead mangled the phrase into what would become their war cry for the day: "RORE MUM!"

When one of them made a great shot you could hear the "RORE MUM!" from three fairways away. Horrendous shots were also followed by the cry, as half the bottle of Mount Gay was consumed by the end of the match, which they somehow won.

"We're going to have to pace ourselves to get through these next two matches," Banes advised Dick.

"Rore mum," Yaprickya replied, taking another slug.

To keep their wits sharp, they decided to place

a side bet for the eighteen holes they still had to play that day. They batted around the idea of most fairways or greens hit in regulation, but yearned for a more creative bet. What they settled on was the least amount of putts with a $20/putt differential. So if Yaprickya had twenty putts and Banes had thirty six, Yaprickya would win $320. They figured it was painful enough to keep them focused on their game.

What made it really interesting was that any putting from off the green didn't count as a putt. So they became the lunatic fringe, always hoping for the apron of the green rather than the center. This mystified their next opponents much like the rum did during their first match, and before they could recover, Banes and Yaprickya duked it out on the greens, and wound up with thirteen putts and fourteen respectively. Not bad for nine holes.

Two matches down, and they had seven points on

the board having won 3-up and 4-up. Dick let out an extremely loud and extenuated "ROOOOORE MUM!" and Banes passed him the bottle shutting him up before the guys on the first tee could come over and shove their Pro V1s in his trap.

"Maybe we ought to double the putting wager on the next nine," Banes suggested.

"You got your ATM card witchoo?" Dick slurred when he finally freed the bottle from his lips. "C'mon, I'll buy you a burger with my future winnings."

They inhaled a couple of obscenely large and rare burgers and then headed to the first tee for their last match of the day. Waiting for them were Cavanaugh and Hedge, who in the last two years had padded their handicaps enough to slide into the same distinguished flight as Banes and Yaprickya.

"Side?" asked Cav as they teed up. "Absolutely," Dick replied and told the guys about the side bet he and Banes had going. They decided they wanted in, and the four of them wound up playing for $40 per putt per team.

"Good luck, girls," Cav said before rocketing one right down the middle. Hedge followed him and sprayed his off to the right into the driving range. "Better reload," he muttered and smacked one right next to Cavanaugh's. "If only I'd done that the first time."

Yaprickya took them out with a ferocious draw that started out over the bunkers on the right side of the fairway and then bent left landing in the center of the short grass twenty yards beyond Cav and Hedge.

Banes came at them from the opposite direction, and sailed a fade to fairway right just short of his partner. That left Cav and Hedge with about 120 yards to the green, Banes with 115, and Dick with only 100.

Cav pureed a wedge, but a tailwind caught it and took it over the green into the back bunker. "Son of a beach!" he cursed. Hedge swung an easy nine and hit it pin high, but hung it out to the right in the four-inch rough.

"Door's open," Dick coached as Banes got ready to hit. But the door slammed shut when Banes shanked it into the fescue.

"Hey Ravi Shankar, stick with the sitar," Dick advised.

"Hey Yaprickya, worry about your own damn ball."

Dick did just that. He hit a dead solid perfect 51° to within three feet. Banes handed him the bottle and dropped another ball hitting a beauty a foot inside of Dick's. "Well, I may not be in the hole, but my putting bet is still alive."

Dick and Banes ham and egged it to go 3-up coming into the last hole, and a putt ahead in the side bet. Cav and Hedge pressed, figuring it's the only shot they have at evening the bet, and the adrenaline surge was palpable.

"You're on, you pathetic low life three-putters," Dick graciously accepted the press.

The finishing hole was a short par four at only 340 yards with a slight dogleg right, but there was plenty of trouble between tee and green. Cav and Hedge played it smart, taking out irons and staking their claim to the fairway. Dick pulled some grass out of the ground and tossed it in the air observing that the wind was behind him. Armed with that newfound knowledge and his Greatest Big Bertha driver, he stepped up to the ball and took a huge whack at it. The ball was beautifully struck, but pulled a tad, and it sailed into the long grass just short and left of the green. *Bertha don't you come around here anymore,* Dick sang into a Callaway microphone.

"Grateful Dead, how appropriate," Hedge said basking in the glee that comes from lying in the fairway with a press riding on the hole.

Banes was about to step up to the tee with a 4-iron, but decided life is too short to practice safe golf. So he went back to his bag for his driver.

"Now you're cooking with gas," his partner said.

Banes took a supercharged practice swing chasing the butterflies away, and then struck the ball with a nice, rhythmic full swing. His Titleist sailed out over the chasm on the right, and then drew back looking like it might actually make the green. Only one thing stood in its way—an immense oak tree.

"Ninety percent air," he prayed, but it was punctuated by the sound of balata striking wood. "Anyone see where that dropped?" he asked, but all he got was shrugged shoulders.

Cav and Hedge were halfway down the fairway

when Banes passed them doing his best Sergio sprint. He scanned the horizon but it was clear his ball wasn't on the fairway or the green. He wandered over to the tree and sitting just to the right of its massive trunk was his ball. "How the hell am I going to get a club on that?" he wanted to say but the only words that came out were, "RORE MUM!"

His opponents hit some well-struck balls and left themselves a couple of long putts for birdie. Dick was hip-deep in the long grass looking for his ball. And Banes stood over his ball wishing he had a left-handed club in his bag.

Only one thing to do.

He took out his Zaap putter and started taking some left-handed practice swings. The Zaap had a two-inch slot on the back of the head that made it easy to scoop up the ball after a putt.

If I strike it just right, I might get lucky.

Dick found his ball and managed to hack it out of the long grass to the fringe of the green. He was a happy man until he saw Banes with the putter.

"What are you, out of your mind?!?"

"Eat me," Banes replied.

Yaprickya just shook his head and said, "I hope you're enjoying the tournament, because it's the last one you're playing in."

"Eat me," Banes repeated before taking a swipe at the ball lefty with the back of the putter sending it shooting out in a low trajectory much hotter than he'd have liked. It slammed into the side of a pot bunker and bounced nearly straight up landing on the green at the top of a tier before cascading slowly down toward the cup where it stopped seven or eight inches from nirvana. Dick just looked at him, and picked up on the newfound phrase, "Eat me." He liked it and latched on to it like it was a mantra that took him one step closer to enlightenment. "Eat me," he repeated, hugging Banes. "EAT ME!"

"YOU DOG YOU," Cavanaugh groused. "You nearly just eagled the damn hole. One of us has to sink this, Hedgie," he said not so much as an observation, but as a command to himself and his partner.

Only problem was his putt had to essentially roll off the green and back on if it was going to have a chance of going in the cup. While he was coming to that realization, Hedge lined up his birdie attempt and was about to putt when Cav said, "Whatever you do, don't leave it short."

It was a good putt, but had just a hair too much steam on it and didn't take all the break and instead rimmed out and came back at Hedge like a boomerang. "How did that not go in?" he wondered.

"Nice prom date putt," Dick said. "All lip and no

hole." Meanwhile he lagged to within a foot and they gave him the rest.

"That's a one putt," he reminded Banes, rubbing in the fact that he'd just won their side bet.

Cavanaugh was well aware of what it meant to their bet, too. He pulled out his lob wedge and with the kind of concentration only a man wearing plaid pants can summon up, hit a high arcing shot that landed two feet beyond the cup and just when Banes and Yaprickya thought they'd won the match, the bet and the press, the ball spun back into the hole with authority.

"YEAH BABY!" Hedge whooped, giving his partner a high five. "We may have lost the match, but we halved the bet and won the press. RORE MUM THAT GIRLS." But the bottle was dry. They made a beeline to the clubhouse to remedy the situation where they sat on the back porch reliving the day and eventually some of the misdeeds they committed while in high school together.

"Remember that night you were out here drinking with Fresno and you accidentally set the rain hut on fire?" Hedge asked Dick.

"Accidentally?" Yaprickya raised an eyebrow. "You should have seen us run when the cops and the entire firehouse descended on us. Fresno didn't really know the lay of the land and ran full bore into one of the pot bunkers on 12. Even over the sirens you could hear the bone in his thigh crack. He spent the next six months in a cast."

"Yeah, and you spent it on probation," Banes reminded him. "You were lucky they didn't lock you up for that stunt."

The conversation meandered until Cavanaugh overheard one of the members talking about this year's gift to the players. "That piece of shit on wheels?" Cav asked none-too-softly. His Irish was clearly up. He thought the suitcase was an abomination, and railed about it until someone said, "Tell us what you really think." So Cav went into the locker room, got his gift and his 9-iron, and re-emerged asking, "You wanna know what I really think?"

With that he started wailing on the suitcase until his club snapped in two. That just pissed him off even more, and much to the delight of the crowd he began kicking the bag and jumping on it until it resembled breakfast at IHOP.

But instead of topping it with maple syrup, he went over to the grill, grabbed the lighter fluid and dragged the flattened suitcase into a neighboring sand trap before dousing it with the fluid. "Anyone got a light?" he asked, and Hedge came to his aid with a match. As the thing burst into flames, the audience burst into applause. Then, one by one, the rest of the Cro-Magnons retrieved their gifts and tossed them into the flames until they had a roaring bonfire of the insanities.

Needless to say, there were some bloodshot eyes around the breakfast table in the morning, but it was all business as the players went to the first tee. Crews had been hard at work for hours already, manicuring the course, cutting the greens and rolling them, and cleaning up the horrific mess the cavemen had made the night before.

Yaprickya and Banes had won all three of their matches Friday, but Saturday morning the weather changed and a steady drizzle threatened to put out their fire. Banes put on a new rain suit. Dick wore a flimsy wind shirt.

By the time they reached the 9th tee in their first match of the day, the wind had shifted into high gear and the rain was coming down sideways. It was a miracle if you could swing the club and keep it from going further than the ball. What turned out to be even more miraculous was that they won the match and were 4 and 0 going into their final battle.

As they waited under a tent at the turn for the last twosome they would play who were a couple of holes behind them, Dick, who was absolutely drenched, looked at Banes and said, "Let's go in."

"What are you crazy?" Probably not the right question to ask a madman like Yaprickya.

"I gotta take a dump," he said. It was somewhat inconvenient in that they were about as far from the clubhouse as you can be.

"There's no time," Banes said. "Hold it till we get done with this last match."

"I'm going to the maintenance shack," Dick insisted before darting off into the woods towards the little building used by the guys who work on the course. The bathroom resembled something out of the movie *Trainspotting*.

The other team arrived, and the three of them

skulked through the rain to the 10th tee without Dick. They waited and waited but there was no sign of him. Polite conversation devolved into derisive jokes. "Maybe it's stuck. Can you imagine shitting out one of those steaks we ate last night?" asked the obstetrician on the team. "Yeah, Doc, go get your forceps and help him out," his partner urged.

They laughed while Banes chewed on his fingernails through his golf glove knowing that if Dickie boy didn't show soon, they'd forfeit the match and have no chance of winning the tournament.

What seemed like a century later, Godot appeared in a yellow poncho that was about five sizes too small for his Flintstonian frame. "Where the Sam Snead have you been?" Banes asked. "And where the hell are your clothes?"

And this is where Dick Yaprickya told a little tale of woe that would go down in the annals of the GC

Golf Club as a fitting sequel to his legendary ball-washer fiasco.

"First thing I saw when I entered the maintenance shack was a microwave. So I stripped down to nothing but my FootJoys and placed my sopping clothes in the oven." The three of them groaned in utter amazement.

Dick continued.

"Since they were light colored, I put it on the poultry setting, and nuked them while I tended to my business. Then I smelled something, and by the time I could get back to the microwave, all that was left was a charred and melted heap."

So here he was on the tenth tee in a borrowed poncho clearly belonging to someone several inches shorter and a few dozen pounds lighter, while the rest of his foursome was busting a gut.

"You can't possibly swing a club in that thing," Banes said and set about figuring out how Yaprickya could play the match. The answer was on his golf bag: an oversized, half-drenched Garden City Golf Club towel he'd had the foresight to pick up in the pro shop that morning.

Dick wrung it out and wrapped it around his waist, securing it with the metal clasp that moments ago held it to Banes' bag, and ditched the poncho. As if on cue, the skies cleared, they teed off, and headed on down the tenth fairway.

As they approached the 18th green with the match all square, a number of golfers were sitting on the clubhouse porch and at the sight of Dick in nothing but a golf towel, they rose to their feet and gave him a standing ovation. He responded by sinking a birdie putt to win the match and the crystal, and then did a little dance in his birthday suit for the crowd, waving the golf towel in the brisk October air.

"Must be cold out there!" someone yelled from the porch.

"Honey, I shrunk my golf score!" Yaprickya yelled back, oblivious to all else.

When Banes arrived home later that night, he handed Gwen a bouquet of roses and this year's prize, a vase with the thistle logo etched on it. She filled the vase, placed it on the mantle, looked at her hubby with adoring eyes and said, "Congratulations Tiger. I knew you could do it."

You know she's right, Banes thought to himself. I do live for this weekend.

ENDLESS SOLSTICE

Skully was full of bright ideas.

First it was the practice round: twenty-seven holes. Kinda like running a half-marathon the day before a marathon.

Then it was the sleepover. Not that it was difficult convincing his playing partners Chester Banes, Dick Yaprickya and Bob Obcorb that this was the thing to do. After all, they did have to get up at 4:30 a.m. to get to the course on time. And Skully's pad was a bachelor's playground. Pool table. Foosball. Pong. Poker. Air hockey. Shuffleboard. Xbox. Darts.

Of course the guys had to play them all.

"We'll call it the Solstice Olympics," declared Banes.

"Ah, so, the S.O." acronymed Obcorb.

"SO there," Yaprickya chimed in.

"SO be it," Skully blessed it.

"It's the perfect counterpoint to the Currituck Winter Olympics," Banes observed, referring to the annual event on the Outer Banks the boys played in every year.

"Now Banes, don't go starting with that counter-point shit again," Skully implored.

"And what's the point of this counter?" asked Yaprickya, sidling up to the bar and knocking on its gleaming walnut surface.

"BARKEEP!" Obcorb shouted, joining his friend at the bar.

"Fill 'er up?" Skully offered, sliding behind the taps. "I bought a keg for the occasion."

"Hey, weekends were made for Michelob," Banes adlibbed.

"They sure aren't made for Michelson," Obcorb added.

"I hadn't realized the weekend began on Tuesday," said Yaprickya.

"Well, this ain't the weekend, and this ain't Michelob," replied Skully, placing a perfectly poured pint of Guinness on the bar. After he had poured four of them he raised his cup in a toast. "May the wind I just broke rise up to meet you."

"Oh, that's cruel," complained Banes waving the air in front of his nose and retreating from the bar.

"Not as cruel as the shellacking Yaprickya and I are going to give you two on the Pong table," Obcorb threw the gauntlet.

"Oh yeah? Skully and I will take you two lightweights on any day," Banes needled Obcorb and

Yaprickya who together tipped the scale at no less than 500 pounds.

"Not so fast now," Skully said removing a River Creek Club hat from a peg on the wall. "Ante up boys."

He passed the hat and they each threw in a silver dollar. They had agreed years ago to play more for honor than gold. It was the kind of agreement that kept friendships in tact while still making the bet interesting. Because they never spent these silver dollars. Their collection of them became a living history of bets gone by, turning the good times they represented into the kind of legal tender they didn't part with lightly.

So the games they played tended to be rather competitive. And this game of pong was no exception. They each placed their full cup of Guinness on the table next to their partner's, centered a paddle's length from the end. If a cup was hit, the hit team drank. If the ball landed in the cup, the owner of the cup had to chug. And if someone knocked one of their opponents' cups over, he had to fill and chug. The point is to knock over the opponents' cups. You don't want to knock over your own.

The game came to an early demise when Banes took a flying leap at a shot Obcorb had lobbed over the net with backspin. From three feet behind the table, Banes lurched forward and launched himself at the ball smashing it back over the net knocking down both his opponents' cups. Only problem was his leap managed to knock down his and Skully's cups too, and the table with it, and both sides had to refill and chug.

Before drinking, Yaprickya held up his cup and toasted Banes' incredible shot.

"He ought to be publicly pissed on. He ought to be publicly shot. And put in a public urinal (pronounced 'your eye null'). And left there forever to rot."

"To rot!" they all repeated and downed their brews in one breathless gulp.

After they'd all refilled, Obcorb inquired, "Foos anyone?"

"Same teams?" Banes asked rhetorically, stepping up to the table and placing his draft near his goal.

"Let's roll," Obcorb declared from the other side of the table, checking the spin on his defensive line. "Any WD-40, Skull?"

Skully reached in a nearby cabinet that also held chalk, talcum, poker chips and assorted other implements of self-destruction, and pulled out a can of the requested lubricant. He sprayed each rod and they were ready to rock.

On the first play of the game, Skully got possession of the ball and kicked it up to his front line.

The three plastic men passed it back and forth and then shot. Obcorb blocked it with his goalie and passed it to one of his fullbacks.

"Here we go," he proclaimed before a lightning-fast shot rocketed down an alley. Skully and Banes were too slow to cover and the ball hit the back of the goal with a boom that filled the room and emptied Banes' full cup of Guinness by freeing it from its precarious perch on the end of the table.

Skully just shook his head and glared at the guys around the room.

"We've been here all of five minutes and you guys have spilled five beers already."

The muscles in his jaw tightened and he squinted his slate blue eyes. It's precisely this kind of visage that usually precedes the phrase, "If looks could kill."

Skully raised an eyebrow and said, "I'm proud of you, men."

He smiled and walked across the stout-laden cement floor past his yellow lab Harp and black lab Guinness who were lapping up the spillage with single-minded focus. In the corner of the room, Skully opened a humidor the size of an orange crate.

"Stogie?"

Everyone partook but Banes, who declined saying, "They keep me up at night."

Turned out the only ones who got any sleep that night were the dogs that were out cold after drinking the beer on the floor.

And it wasn't a cigar that kept Banes up, but a game of poker that lasted nearly till dawn. In the grand scheme of things, it was a rather harmless game. Before the silver dollar rule, there were nights when car keys appeared in the kitty, mingled with hundreds of dollars and piles of chips worth hundreds more.

But now they limited themselves to $110 apiece. One hundred in Sacagawea dollars plus ten in silver dollars that were reserved for special challenges.

At five a.m. they were in the middle of an Acey/Deucey game that was burning everybody who tried to take the pot. The pot continued to swell until Banes pulled a deuce and an ace.

"What do you think? Should I risk more than a dollar?" he asked his fellow card players.

"No risk, no reward," Yaprickya advised.

"No balls, no dolls," Obcorb obscured.

"Fortune sides with those who dare," Skully said in his best Confucius accent.

"Hell, life is short," Banes made his decision. "Pot."

With that, another deuce came up, and Banes was suddenly down to his last silver dollar.

"And death is long," he said, putting a mass of coins in the middle of the table.

"Speaking of hell, we gotta go," realized Skully looking at his watch.

"What about the game?" Yaprickya grumbled through a gnawed-up smoked-down stogie-filled mouth.

"We'll finish it tonight," Skully declared. "After all, it is the longest day of the year."

"Make that the longest two days," observed Obcorb.

They had thrown their clubs in Skully's Jeep the night before along with a change of clothes, a case of water, assorted flasks, boxes of balls, a tube of Ben Gay and bottles of sunscreen, aloe, Advil and Aleve.

"Anything we're forgetting?" Skully asked as he engaged the ignition.

"Our sanity," was the only reply that came to mind.

Half an hour later they were sucking down coffee sitting in their carts at Bull Run in the pre-dawn light. As the carts got under way, Banes raised his coffee cup to his playing partners, "May the course be with you."

For the next thirteen hours, they played the course three times. They started out loose after being up all night. By the second round, they were dragging their tails. And by the third, they'd found themselves immersed in a zombie-like second wind that stuck with them till the end of the Solstice.

When they got to the 54th hole, there were pervasive sighs of relief from the motley crew that had somehow survived three rounds in a day after an all-nighter and twenty-seven holes the previous day.

"Last hole, boys," Skully announced.

"Thank God," groaned Yaprickya.

"Yeah, now we can get back to our Acey/Deucey game," added Obcorb.

"C'mon guys," Banes pleaded. "The last thing I want to do is sit back down at that card table. I'll never get up."

"Why don't we play this hole for what's in the pot?" suggested Skully.

"Capital idea, Skull," Yaprickya patted his friend on the back.

"I'm in," said Obcorb.

"But there must be $300 in there, not to mention all those silver dollars," Banes objected. "We're gonna wager that on one lousy par three when we can barely swing a club anymore?"

"Precisely," Skully affirmed.

"Then pass the swing lube," Banes caved, taking his flask out of his bag and imbibing a healthy swig of Knockando single malt before handing it to Skully who followed suit and passed it along.

Banes then teed it up and hit his best shot of the day, a magnificent 7-iron with a slight draw

that landed on the right side of the green and proceeded to roll left stopping a foot and a half from
the pin.

"That must be some pretty good schwing lube,"
Yaprickya opined reaching for the flask and taking
a long pull.

Skully then shot and left it in the greenside bunker. Obcorb's landed in the rough just off the putting surface. Then Yaprickya got up and shanked
his into the woods.

"Son of a prickya," he yelled and winged his club
toward the green. It made a chopper-like whoop-
ing sound as it zeroed in on its target, hit the pin
with a loud clang, and the club head dropped into
the hole.

"Well I'll be a monkey's funkin' uncle," Skully
declared.

"Who needs balls?" Yaprickya asked, jumping in
the cart.

He got to the green and extracted his 8-iron from the cup, repairing the damage it did to the lip as best he could.

"Somebody chip her in," he implored. "Even Banes can't miss that putt."

Skully made a half-decent sand shot, but left himself a twenty-foot putt for par.

Obcorb chipped close, narrowly missing the hole and lamenting, "Ooh, that would have been schweet." The ball came to rest about the same distance to the hole as Banes'.

"Well, I guess that's that," Yaprickya said with an air of finality while he pulled the pin. "Knock her in Banes."

Banes stood over his ball and the green started spinning like a merry-go-round. Doing his best to ignore it, he brought the putter head back and tapped the ball into the cup. Only it didn't go in. It boomeranged off the wounded lip, and wound up further from the hole than it had started.

"Oh my gawd," Yaprickya moaned with delight.

"Took the words right out of my mouth," Banes said dejectedly, marking his ball.

"Good, good?" Skully said to Banes and Obcorb who would tie the hole at three.

"Okay by me," Obcorb replied. "I'd hate to see Banes miss two gimme putts in a row."

Which was the wrong thing to say. Banes, who was about to agree to the half, instead put his ball down and picked up his last remaining silver dollar which was serving as his ball marker.

"And I'd hate to deprive you of an opportunity to lose the hole," he fired back at Obcorb.

As Banes stood over his ball and took a practice swing, he thought of all the glorious coins sitting back on the poker table. As he did so, the merry-go-round started up again but this time he went along for the ride. Only he felt more like a polo player than a golfer as he putted, and his ball again found the lip of the cup, did a 360 and threatened to come right back to him.

"DROP!" he shouted at it from the saddle of his wooden horse. The ball sat on the lip for what seemed like an eternity before obeying its master and dropping into the abyss.

"YES!" Banes swung his fist in the air while dismounting the merry-go-round which had come to a screeching halt. He bent down to pluck his ball from the cup and muttered, "Take that you lousy hole."

"Nice putt Banes. All right Bobby," Yaprickya encouraged Obcorb. "Slap it in."

"Yeah, pard, back of the cup," Skully joined in, forming a united front.

Obcorb lined up the short putt. "Piece of cake." He took a stab at the ball and it never had a chance. "Piece of crap," he revised.

"Guess that's it," said Banes as he picked up the pin with a shit-eating grin.

"AHEM," Skully pointed to his ball mark, reminding his opponent that he was still in the hole. "The rumors of my death are greatly exaggerated."

"My bad," Banes admitted. "My bad."

Obcorb and Yaprickya came to Skully's aid dishing out their read on his twenty-foot putt. Between the three of them, they had as many different reads.

"When in doubt, trust your gut," Skully said under his breath to an audience of one as he stood over the ball. He inhaled deeply, took the putter back, and followed through keeping his head still while his heart raced and the ball somersaulted across the dance floor taking the break until it was clear the only place it could possibly wind up was in the cup.

"REPLAY!" Yaprickya cheered, back in the game.

"Who's better than you?" Obcorb high-fived the man of the minute.

Banes shook his head, reached into the cup for Skully's ball, tossed it back to him and replaced the pin while exclaiming, "Helluva putt."

"Two tie, all tie," Skully meditated on a new mantra.

The sun sank lower on the horizon casting a warm light on the green as the boys went back to the tee. The group behind them was just finishing their last hole, so playing the par three again wouldn't pose a problem.

So they played the hole again. And two tied. And again. And two tied. And again. And two tied. And again and again and again. And two tied each time.

"This isn't the Solstice, it's Groundhog Day," Yaprickya shouted after the 63rd hole.

"Yeah, and Punxsutawney Phil won't be seeing his shadow in this light," Obcorb uttered through the twilight.

"I'm more concerned with seeing dinner," growled Banes. "While we're out here hacking up this hole in the dark, the rest of the tournament is inside enjoying a good meal."

"All you gotta do is win the hole, Banes, and you can buy us all a nice dinner," said Skully. "In the meantime, I'm going to grab the car so we can shine a little light on the green. To the parking lot, Banes."

Banes hopped back in the cart and made a beeline through the encroaching nightfall to the parking lot where they picked up Skully's Jeep. He was tempted to stop in the clubhouse and grab some food, but was afraid he might get comfortable and decide to stay. And then all those dollars lying on the poker table would just slip from his grasp. As he drove back to the battleground with Skully following in the Jeep, his resolve became so steely it left a metallic taste in his mouth. Which, of course, was all the motivation he needed for another shot of Knockando.

"I saw that," said Skully jumping out of the Jeep as they pulled to a halt by the tee box. His smoky baritone broke into song: *"Don't Bogart that flask, my friend. Pass it over to me."*

Banes tossed the flask to his buddy and grabbed his 7-iron. Again.

Obcorb and Yaprickya were lying on the tee box either looking at the stars or catching forty winks, he couldn't tell.

"Rise and shine boys, it's show time," Skully declared putting on the high beams.

"I've fallen and I can't get up," moaned Yaprickya.

"Call 911," Obcorb added. "I think my ticker's stopped tickin'."

"Get a Timex," Banes told him, "because you're about to take a lickin'."

With that he teed it up and took a determined swing that sent his ball soaring through the head-lamp-lit sky.

"Oh Banes, you've struck gold with this one," Skully said through a dropped jaw.

"It's dead on," Obcorb agreed.

"CLANG," rang the pin as the ball struck it and ricocheted hard off the metal and into the bunker.

"WHAT!?!" Banes gasped.

"Ah, you were robbed," Yaprickya commiserated.

No one else got a good shot off, and the green was left without a ball on it.

Skully, Yaprickya and Obcorb all chipped on, and the safe bet would be that they would all make three or all make four, because it was almost inconceivable that one of them would finally win the hole.

"Good, good, good?" Skully laid a peace offering on the table to see if they could just concede their putts and head back to the tee for a 65th hole.

Yaprickya and Obcorb were quick to accept, and picked up their balls. Banes had already climbed into the bunker, so he took a whack at his ball that was half-buried in the sand. It came out a little hot, but had a good line and once again smacked into the pin with a tinny CLANG.

Only this time, there was no ricochet. The ball dropped straight down and settled in the cup where it would stay until Banes fished it out while his opponents writhed in agony on the sidelines.

Now it was Banes' turn to break into song. *"Well, uh, everybody heard about the bird, I said a bird, bird, bird, bird is a word."*

He used the pin as a microphone and did a little hippy shake as the headlights became spotlights illuminating the rising star on the green dance floor.

"Well you didn't get the ace," Skully wryly observed, "but you did get the deuce. And that's good enough for the pot."

"Drinks are on me boys," Banes said accepting a cigar from Obcorb.

They put their clubs in Skully's Jeep and left the golf carts there at the scene of the crime.

"They'll hate us for that in the morning," said Yaprickya.

"No they won't," countered Banes, sticking a $20 in each of the cupholders.

Consciences clear, they drove off the course and back towards Skully's place. On the ride home, Dick and Bob fell asleep in the backseat and kept Skully and Banes awake with their ear-blasting snores.

"HAAWNK. SHHOOO."

"How do their wives tolerate that?" wondered Banes.

"HAAWWNNKK. SHOOOOOOOOO."

"Separate beds?"

"HUHUHUHAAAWWWNNNKKK."

"Separate rooms would be more like it."

"SHOOOOOOHOOOOHOOO."

"Maybe separate homes."

When they pulled into Skully's driveway they tried to wake the sleeping giants, but it was no use. They lowered the windows so they wouldn't suffocate, and left them to their own devices in dreamland.

"I hope the neighbors don't complain about the decibel level," Banes said stumbling toward the house.

When Skully opened the door Harp and Guinness nearly knocked him over as they barreled through the doorway to the great outdoors.

"They really had to go," Banes noticed.

"Speaking of which, I could use a shower," Skully said. "Make yourself at home."

Banes took him up on his invitation and headed straight for the kitchen. He was too tired to prepare anything, so he grabbed Cheez-Its for himself and Bonz for Harp, figuring the dog must be hungry, too.

On the way to one of Skully's inviting sofas, Banes let Harp back in before plopping on the couch. He turned on the tube, found the Golf Channel to see if his shot out of the sand had made the highlights, and began to stuff his face with his favorite snack cracker. Harp nudged him with her nose, so he fed her some Bonz in between shoveling Cheez-Its into his pie hole.

Skully appeared a few minutes later and plunked down a pillowcase loaded with the loot that had been on the poker table.

"Your winnings," he said.

"You're a gentleman and a scholar, Skull," Banes thanked him. "Care for a Cheez-It?"

Banes handed Skully the package after grabbing a handful and popping a few in his mouth.

"Are they good?" Skully wanted to know.

"A bit stale, but I'm so hungry I could eat a horse right now," Banes replied.

"That's good, because that's about what you're eating at the moment Banes," Skully said. "Or should I call you Bonz?"

Skully shoved the package of dog treats in his friend's face while Banes chewed without interruption.

"You know, these are pretty good," Banes admitted, nonplussed. "Maybe even better than Cheez-Its."

The two of them spent the next hour watching Golf Central and eating doggie snacks.

When the box was empty, Banes decided it was time to head home before he was in the doghouse with his wife Gwen. He was still clutching the empty bag of Bonz as he turned to Skully and said, "Funny, I've got a sudden urge to bury this box in the backyard."

On his way out the door, Banes heard Skully's parting shot, "Well it's a good thing you can't lick your balls."

ONE IN A MILLION

Every September, the boys rallied around the flag-poles at Lowes Island Club for the National Capital Golf Classic, an annual benefit for the American Cancer Society's prostate cancer efforts.

Banes served on the organizing committee, and was given two slots for his work on the tournament's behalf. His firm did the advertising for the event. This year, the ad featured a shot of a guy holding up a 6-iron toward the camera and some copy that read, "One in six men get it. Fight prostate cancer with a club."

Close to fifty foursomes turned out to do just

that, each paying the generous $5500 entrance contribution. It was always a high-class event, with valet parking, player gifts like new FootJoys, leather garment bags, individually tailored golf slacks, and Sea Island cotton golf shirts. And big prizes, like cars for holes-in-one on each of the par threes. Not to mention golf on not one, but two of the sweetest golf courses in the Mid-Atlantic. There was Tom Fazio's Island Course, the club's original gem, and the newer Arthur Hills designed River Course.

Banes enlisted his buddy Skully to play, and they were teamed with Dogtrack and Chili Dip, a couple of friends who ran companies that donated printing for the Golf Classic brochures and post-ers. After a leisurely breakfast on the back patio, the players made their way to the carts. Jim, the tournament chairman, thanked the players for coming, and then Bob, Lowes Island's head pro, explained the rules.

It was an idyllic September morning except for one small thing. A stiff wind was blowing upriver that promised to mess with the best of shots. The breeze also made it hard to hear everything Jim and Bob said, because it was blowing so loud into the microphone. Bob told the players that this year, the tournament was a scramble format, but between the wind and Skully telling a lewd joke about going to a lady doctor for a prostate exam, Banes' foursome missed that directive and wound up playing their own balls as they'd done in previous years. Their problems were compounded when their foursome was relegated to the River Course, the more difficult of the two Lowes Island tracks.

"All right boys, we're off," Banes said to his crew.

"Like the bride's pajamas," Skully added, as they piloted their carts down toward the links along the Potomac. *"Take me to the river,"* he sang off key.

When they got to the first tee, Dogtrack, the best player in their foursome, tried to get in their pockets. "Dollar skins?"

"As long as we factor in handicaps," Chili Dip, the twenty-one-going-on-sixteen, said.

"Good by me," Banes agreed.

"Junk?" asked Skully. "Birdies, greenies, sandies and barkies?"

"What no polies?" Banes asked back.

"What the Funk's a polie?" Dogtrack wanted to know.

"That's when you're shooting for the green and hit the flagstick," Banes replied.

"And you immediately sprout a woodie," Skully added.

"Speaking of woodies, why don't you whip yours out and show us the way," said Chili.

"Yeah, grip it and rip it, Skull."

"Ouch," Skully said pulling the driver from his

bag, walking up to the box, inserting a tee in the ground, a ball on the tee, and a swing on the ball in one continuous motion. The 1st hole on The River Course requires a fairly straight tee shot to thread through the trees bracketing a marsh and onto the fairway 170 or so yards beyond. Skully started his shot off to the right and collided with a large syca- more which sent his ball directly back at the tee box making Skully dance the Macarena to save his ankles as he let out a battle cry. "INCOMING!"

"Nice shot, Ace," said Chili usurping the box from him.

"Hey, I drew first blood though. That, Dipper, was a first-class barkie. ARF! ARF!" Skully barked and started humping Chili Dip's leg.

"Down boy." When he broke free, Chili took his time acting out a pre-shot routine that struck them all as a bit excessive for a hack with a 21 handicap. His movements were careful, deliberate, and bordering on downright slow, that is until he got to his downswing, which was a lightning bolt.

The ball was topped into the hazard. "Guess I kinda rushed that swing."

"You freakin' Limbaughed it," Dogtrack said. "Bad day to give up Oxycontin."

"That shot was simply an oxymoron, Dog," said Chili.

"Nothing that a shot of this can't cure," Banes said tossing his flask.

"Guess it's five o'clock somewhere," Chili said unscrewing the cap. It was 10:30 in Virginia.

Banes took the box and put a sweet swing on the ball sending it to the middle of the fairway. Dog-track followed suit, as did Chili Dip and Skully after re-teeing.

Dog and Banes both parred the hole, pushing the skin to the next hole, a short par four that was drivable if you hit a monster.

"No guts, no story," Banes said reaching for Bertha, his driver.

He crushed the ball and it looked like it was going to be perfect until the squall coming off the Potomac knocked it down into the pond in front of the green.

He glared coming off the tee box and did his best *Cuckoo's Nest* Nicholson. "Well at least I tried."

Learning from Banes' mistake, Dog and Dip both hit irons out into the fairway.

But Skully was in the *Cuckoo's Nest* mindset, and approached the tee like the Chief approaching the water cooler in the movie.

He took his stance over the ball and slowly took his driver back imagining the Chief straining to lift the drinking fountain from its mooring. At the top of his swing, all he could see was the Chief lifting with all his might. As he started his downswing, the fountain was freed from its mooring, and as his club hit the ball, all Skully could think of was the Chief hurtling the fountain through the window of the asylum and clearing a gateway to freedom.

And Skully's ball, like the Chief, took full advantage of that gateway, and rocketed skyward. It started toward fairway right and then the wind took hold of it. While it was still gaining velocity, the wind helped out with direction and pushed it toward the water and the green. It seemed to hang for an eternity up in the blue sky laced with swift clouds before it started its descent. Would it be the drink or the green?

The ball came down just short and hit a rock at the water's edge, which sent it shooting back up in the air fifty feet. It did a number of somersaults in the wind and touched down safely ten feet from the pin.

"Nice rockie," Dip said. "That's good for a buck."

"Tigerific," Banes high-fived Chief Skully and

passed him the flask. Skully did a fist pump with one hand and raised the flask with the other, basking in the warmth of the single malt.

"Mmm. Juicy Fruit."

Skully proceeded to miss his birdie putt, Chili halved the hole with a par, and they carried the skins to another hole. And another. And another and another.

Then they came upon a long par five and were greeted by Kathryn from the Cancer Society at the tee.

"All right boys, pony up twenty dollars and you can tee off from the red tees."

The boys weighed the cash outlay against the fifty-yard advantage the ladies tee would give them. With so many skins on the line, it was a no-brainer.

"I'm in," they said in unison.

"All right, put these on," Kathryn said, tossing

some horrid floral skirts, muumuus and tutus, their way.

The boys groaned as they considered the prospect of dressing in drag.

Skully started to drop his trousers, and Banes started humming the old Noxema stripper tune.

"I appreciate the cheap thrill, boys, but you can put them on over your pants," Karen suggested.

Skully finished dressing and sashayed up to the ladies' tee.

"Does this skirt make my butt look fat?" he said standing over the ball and sticking out his tail like a silverback gorilla in heat.

He took a King Kong swing and put his ball within striking distance of the hole. Banes took a picture that captured Skully's beautiful swing and attire.

"Nice shot you sexy thing," he said showing the others the picture on his digital camera.

"Here, let me take one of the four of you," Karen said and snapped a shot of them.

As she did, the wind gusted and blew up Skully's skirt making him look like Marilyn Monroe in *Bus Stop*. Well, not quite.

They gave Kathryn their skirts and twenty dollars a man for the pleasure of wearing them.

"Thanks. Good luck girls," Kathryn said, sending them on their way.

Only Dog and Skully had a shot at reaching the green in two. Chili had donated two to the woods on the left already, and Banes had found a clump of trees to the right.

Dog was lying about 205 yards from the green, and took out a 4-iron. His approach was right on target, and with the wind helping it, the ball found the right front of the green.

Skully had about 195, and elected to hit a 5-iron. Unfortunately for him, when he struck the ball, the wind started swirling and knocked his ball into the greenside bunker. When Skully got to it, he noticed it was half-buried.

"Nice fried egg," Dogtrack said, marking his ball on the green.

"I shall have breakfast in the desert!" Skully proclaimed, wrapped his head in his Tommy Bahama golf towel, and descended into the sand like Lawrence of Arabia. He opened his stance, planted his feet firmly in the beach, opened the face of his sand wedge and emptied his mind. Skully took a big swing and managed to excavate the ball and a bucket of sand up onto the green. The sand storm obscured Skully's vision so he never saw the ball take two hops on the green before burrowing into the cup.

"Where'd it go?" he asked wide-eyed from the trap. There was no sign of the ball.

Dog just shook his head and mumbled, "Lucky

bastard," before pulling it from the hole and tossing it to Skully.

As he lined up his eagle putt to halve the hole,
Chili and Banes offered their encouragement.

"Put 'er in, partner."

"Back of the cup, Dogbreath."

And it might have gotten there, had it not collided with a small pyramid of sand between the ball
and the cup. Skully had not only snookered Dog by
putting his bunker shot in the hole, but by leaving
an obstacle on the green in the process.

The ball stopped an inch short of its ultimate
destination. Rarely is a birdie such sweet sorrow.

"Man, that was for a boatload of skins," Chili
said.

"Don't forget the junk," said Skully of Arabia in
his turban. "Let's see, the eagle's worth a couple,
and then it was a sandy, too." It was if he'd struck
oil in the desert.

"I am the Sultan, I am the Sultan of Schwing," he sang, parodying Dire Straits.

The following hole was a 191-yard par three along the Potomac with a brand new Toyota Highlander sitting near the tee for anyone putting an ace on his card.

With the headwind coming upriver, it played more like 240.

Skully unsheathed his 3-wood and in one fluid motion walked to the box, put a tee in the ground and put a swing on the ball that comes with the confidence of a pocketful of skins.

"Here comes the P.E.F.U.," Chili whispered to the others, referring to the dreaded post-eagle-f#°k-up.

But the ball had other ideas. It cut through the wind like a Ginsu through Land O' Lakes, and headed straight for the pin.

"You gotta be kiddin' me," Dog's jaw dropped.

"Best I've seen all day," said the volunteer monitoring the hole-in-one hole.

The ball came down and knocked the pin like a right from Ali, uprooting it from the hole. The pin collapsed on the green, down for the count. Its flag flopped in the wind signaling surrender. But no one on the tee box could tell where the ball wound up.

"We better check this out," said the volunteer, and they all hopped in their carts and made their way to the green.

Skully, was first to get there. "Damn!"

"Close, but no cigah," Banes said.

"Oh I don't know about that," said Dog, pulling out a small humidor from his bag. He opened it and offered Skully a torpedo.

Skully clipped off the end of the cigar, and said philosophically, "Well, I didn't get the car, but I believe that's a polie."

"And a greenie, and most likely a birdie," Chili added.

"I believe you now have more skins than Dan Snyder," Banes said while offering his friend a light with a windproof jet of blue butane.

When the round was over, the team was out of the money, but Skully was swimming in it. As they were settling up at the bar high above the Potomac, the head pro showed up and told Skully to get out to the 18th fairway.

"What's going on?" Skully asked him.

"You got closest to the pin on number twelve," Bob said. "You're in a shoot-out for a million dollars."

"WHAT?!?"

"You and two other guys get to hit from 165 yards out on the 18th hole of the Island Course. If you hole your shot, you get a million bucks."

"*Here comes your 18th nervous breakdown,*" Banes sang.

107

"Who wants to be a millionaire?" Chili asked, putting his arm around Skully.

Skully finished his drink in a single gulp and followed Bob out to the battleground.

The other two golfers were already down there.

"Do we get a practice shot?" Skully asked.

"You can each have one," Bob told the contestants.

They each hit a shot to help them gauge the club selection and the wind.

Skully's wound up in the bunker to the right of the green.

"I'm afraid I may need a lifeline," he said to his foursome.

"Just summon up whatever mojo helped you hole out that bunker shot," Banes said.

"Should I wear the towel on my head?"

"You don't need it. What club you using?"

Skully held out his 6-iron, and it dawned on

Banes that the scene looked very much like the one depicted in the ad he did for the tournament. So much so, it sent a chill down his spine.

"That's perfect," he said.

The first contender got up and hit a good shot, but the wind pushed it right of the green.

The second was a bit too pumped, and pull-hooked his ball into the trees left of the green.

Then it was Skully's turn. Before swinging, he did a little yoga to stretch his body and calm his mind.

Dogtrack took a swig off his beer and bellowed, "Be the cahone, Skully."

Skully brought his 6-iron back rhythmically, hips turning, arms reaching for the sky, shoulders turning one way and then the other as the club head came down in an angelic arc until its well-worn grooves caught the ball square on the sweet spot sending it flying forward and upward where it battled with the wind, holding its head with a slight draw while it seemingly sat up there, defying gravity, for a brief but brilliant moment before its fall from heaven back to God's green earth below where it settled miraculously into the hole, nothing but cup.

There was a moment of silence followed by a roar that grew deafening as each moment passed. Skully turned in slow motion to face Banes, wide-eyed and incredulous. Banes reciprocated by tackling his friend in a bear hug while shouting "YES" to the high heavens. They rolled in the fairway rejoicing while Dog and Chili showered them with beer.

At the awards dinner that evening, Northern Virginia's latest millionaire was called to the podium by Kathryn to tell the crowd what he was going to do with his newfound riches.

Skully was glowing when he arrived at the mike.

"How schweet it is," he said to jeers, catcalls and applause. "First I want to say thanks to my friend Banes for inviting me to this great and glorious tournament."

Banes stood up and took a bow while the crowd applauded.

"You know," he continued, "it's not every day you get to go out, play a great course with good friends, and—"

"And win a million bucks!" Danny interrupted.

"And win a million bucks," Skully admitted, "and also do something worthwhile, like raise a quarter million bucks for prostate cancer programs."

The crowd applauded and cheered.

"Well, I'd like to make it even more worthwhile," Skully continued. "I'm going to donate half my winnings to the American Cancer Society. Kathryn, a breast cancer survivor herself, started crying and wrapped her arms around Skully as the whole room went up for grabs.

"You're one in a million, Skully," she whispered in his ear.

THE FALL BRAWL

Word spread quickly that Skully had won a million bucks at the American Cancer Society tournament. By the time he and Banes got back to River Creek that evening, a posse had gathered on Skully's front porch. Fred even managed to dig up a Regis Philbin mask and led the group in a chant when the boys pulled into the driveway.

"WHO WANTS TO BE A MILLIONAIRE?" they cried in unison.

"I do, I do," Skully said sliding out of his Jeep.

He was greeted by high fives, fist punches, back slaps, wet kisses and a friendly goose as he made his way through the crowd to his front door.

"The bar is now open," he said, turning the key. As he opened the door, Skully was nearly knocked over by Harp, his yellow lab, who jammed a cold nose in his crotch before setting off to work the crowd. They all followed Skully down to his basement. The room was filled with a celebratory energy.

"You'd think the Redskins had won the Super Bowl," Banes said sliding behind the taps. "Guinness, Harp, or Skully's Homebrew?" He fielded requests and soon everyone had a cup in hand.

"To Skully, proud owner of one millllllllllion dollars," Fred said raising his glass and abandoning his Regis Philbin impersonation in favor of Mike Myer's Dr. Evil.

Gwen was busy at the stereo and soon the band Bare Naked Ladies was singing "If I Had a Million Dollars." She then asked the question that was on everyone's mind. "So Skully, what are you going to do with your newfound riches?"

"One millllllllion dollars," Dr. Evil repeated.

Skully took a sip of his brew and pondered the question.

"Well, first of all, it's only half a million," he said.

A collective "Huh?" rose from the crowd.

"You guys make a pit stop in Vegas between Lowes Island and here?" Gwen asked.

"Skully gave half of his winnings to the Cancer Society," Banes clarified.

"Half a millllllllion dollars," Dr. Evil changed his tune.

Glasses were again held high for Skully and he got a tearful hug from a neighbor who'd lost her husband to cancer in the past year. "That's the sweetest thing," she said before giving him a big kiss.

"Schweet!" Banes said, and a number of their golf buddies echoed, "Schweet!"

"That's awesome, Skully, but my question still stands," said Gwen.

"I haven't really given it much thought," he said. "Maybe buy a vacation home."

"But where would you rather be than here?" Fred asked. "We've got great golf, a pool, tennis courts…"

"Potomac River, Goose Creek, boating, fishing," Gwen continued.

"Not to mention a few friends," Banes added. Shouts of affirmation filled the air.

"I can almost feel your hands in my pockets already," said Skully.

"Hey Skully, who let the bird out of the cage," Banes flapped his middle finger flipping his friend a flying bird.

"Maybe you could retire and play golf for a living," someone said.

"Start training for the Senior Tour."

"That's Champions Tour now."

"As much as I love the game, I think I'd be bored to tears if that's all I did. Besides, a half million doesn't go as far as it used to."

"A half a millllllllllion dollars."

"You know this homebrew of yours goes down like Linda Lovelace," Banes said.

Gwen kneed her husband in the family jewels, but also saw the wisdom of his remark.

"Maybe you could market your beer," she suggested. "It is awfully good."

"My wife has a point there Skull," Banes said. "Not to mention a boney knee." He rubbed his crotch.

"I believe you boys even have a name for it," Gwen said. "What do you call it, Swing Lube?"

"Schwing Lube," Skully and Banes said in unison.

"Schwing Lube, eh? Kind of a mouthful, if you ask me," said Gwen. "How 'bout just 'Schwing'?

"Yeah, Schwing, that's not half bad," said Banes with his ad guy hat on. "Of thee I Schwing."

"It's got my Schwing vote," said Skully before breaking into song. "*Schwing low, schweet chariot…*"

"*Comin' for to carry me home*," Banes joined in, and soon the whole basement was filled with raucous off-key voices. "*Schwing low, schweet chariot, comin' for to carry me home.*"

The following morning, Skully awoke to the slow realization that he was a half a million dollars richer. Through the fog of excess Schwing Lube, a song reverberated in his head, eventually making its way to his vocal chords.

"*If I were a rich man, yadadadadadadadadadadadadadadah.*" The lyrics were just beyond his reach from his perch on the couch where he'd passed out at four a.m. Suddenly a tongue was licking his face.

"Good morning to you, too, Harp," he said to his

yellow dog. Then another tongue appeared, and Guinness joined in on the slobbering.

Just then the front door burst open and Banes appeared singing a little ditty to the tune of something Gene Kelly and later Fred Rogers used to croon.

"Good morning, good morning, it's nice to stay up late. Good morning, good morning to you."

The tune was short-lived, and Banes bellowed "Get your ass out of bed, you lucky stiff, there's work to be done."

"But my ass isn't in bed."

"Well, get it out of whatever sling it's in and rally. We've got a company to launch, a beer to brew, thirsts to slake."

"What, no dragons to slay?" Skully sat up and ran his hands through his hair, making sure his head was still in one piece.

"Here, drink this in remembrance of Schwing."

With that, he handed his friend a venti Starbucks.

"Ah, you're a lifesaver, partner."

"I've got it," Banes said, waving a sheet of paper.

"What's that, a hangover?"

"Nope, hair of the dog." Harp barked at the name of his species. Banes handed the paper to Skully.

"What have we here?" Skully looked down and saw what could be none other than a label design for his beer.

"Pretty schweet," he said to his friend. "When did you cook this up?"

"'Bout four a.m. You like?"

"I love. Looks like we're in business, partner."

"So you do remember."

"Don't mean a thing . . ."

"If it ain't got that Schwing."

"You know," Skully said, "before we put our noses to the barley stone, we should do a little market research."

"Great livers think alike," Banes said. "And you know what's happening next week?"

"Columbus Day sale at Golfdom?"

"Try the Fall Brawl."

"Holy schmokes, I'd nearly forgotten."

"You probably also forgot that Columbus always preferred Myrtle Beach to Plymouth Rock."

"What better venue for a little market research for our Schwing brew."

"Precisely. The Fall Brawl. Four days of nonstop golf with sixteen thirsty golfers."

"We better start brewin'." Skully took a pull off his Starbucks and rose from the couch.

Twelve cases and seven hours later, they pulled up to Caledonia Golf and Fish Club in Pawley's Island, South Carolina, with minutes to spare before their one p.m. tee time.

"Well if it isn't my long-lost brother-in-law," Vinny said as they drove up to the first tee. "Howahya, Banes?"

"Hey, I'm married to your sister, how do you think I am?" Banes said and gave Vinny a bear hug.

Vinny hugged Skully too, and said, "Guys, this is Ricky, one of my oldest friends from Southie."

"Howahya?" Ricky greeted Skully and Banes.

"Anothah Bahston gahlfah, eh?" Banes said doing his best Kennedy accent.

"Belly up to the bah in Hahvahd Yahd," Skully

said, offering a Schwing to each of the guys.

"To the Brawl!" They all tapped their bottles together in a spirited chink.

"Nothing like a little Schwing before you schwing," Banes said.

"This is good schtuff," Vinny said. "Nevva had it befoa."

"That's because we just brewed it," Skully said.

"Sweet."

"We brought a dozen cases," Banes added.

"Even schweetah."

That evening the gang of sixteen managed to put away four cases sitting on the beach catching up with each other. Dick Yaprickya had just pulled in after driving all day from New York, and managed to down half a case by himself.

"Here's to the girl with the little red shoes," he toasted after opening his eleventh Schwing. "She likes her nookie, she likes her booze. She lost her cherry, but that's no sin. She's still got the box that the cherry came in."

Everybody drank to the girl in the red shoes until Larry, also known as "The Vig," called everyone's attention to an easel bearing a few charts.

"Now listen up, losers, here are the bets, the schedule of play, the rules of the game, and the leader board."

"Take me to your leader board," Banes said in an alien voice.

"Banes, here you are on the leader board, right down at the bottom after your questionable play today."

"After we packed the car full of Schwing, there wasn't any room for Banes' game," Skully said.

"As long as there was room for his wallet," Bimbo said. Bimbo had gotten his name because he's a chick magnet. Though not your garden variety. The chicks Bimbo attracted usually sported bottled blonde hair and the IQ of a walnut.

"Got it," Banes said to Bimbo, pulling his wallet out of his pocket and holding it up in the salty air. He then opened up the billfold to reveal his stash of cash. "And at least mine is filled with something other than condoms."

The Vig interrupted the ensuing laughter to bring their attention back to the easel. "I'm glad to see you brought plenty of cabbage, Banes, you may need it. At any point in time during the Brawl, there are at least three bets going on." He went on to explain the Ryder Cup bet, the two-man team bet, the individual bet, and the closest to the pin bets. "Of course side bets are permitted too. Enter at your own risk."

As The Vig finished up holding court on the rules of The Brawl, an overloaded pizza delivery guy arrived carrying a stack of sixteen boxes.

Skully went over to help the guy, and when he took half the boxes away, it revealed that the delivery guy wasn't a guy at all. Her cleavage rose above the remaining boxes like a soaring bird, her blond hair forming wings of peroxide plumage.

"Here, let me help you with those," Bimbo said reaching for the remaining boxes.

"BIMBO! BIMBO!" a number of the guys chanted.

The delivery girl looked hurt. Bimbo saw his opening and took her aside, explaining that "Not all men are able to recognize intelligence when it comes packaged with beauty…" His words trailed off as they walked down the beach.

The following morning was shrouded with fog as the Brawlers made their way to the first tee at The Dunes Golf and Beach Club.

By the 2nd hole, Banes had sat on his prescription glasses that he'd laid on the seat of the golf cart while applying some sunscreen. Not only did he break the lenses, but he punctured a hole in his keister that left a red blotch the size of a dime, that grew to a nickel, and then a quarter, and then a half dollar, and by the time he made it to the next tee, it was the size of a silver dollar.

"Hey Banes, your ass is bleeding," Yaprickya observed.

"Yestaday his game, today his ass," said Vinny.

"Sat on my glasses," said Banes. "Could you watch this for me?"

He took a swipe at the fuzzy object on the tee and looked down the fairway in vain. "Never saw it."

"And you nevva will," said Vinny. "Duckhooked it into the wata."

"Nice shot Mr. Magoo," Skully offered his condolences.

And for the next seven holes Banes played like Ray Charles, only without the smile.

"You know, when your game walks out on you,

it's as if your best girl has just run off with your best friend. And swiped your golf clubs as well. It's not a pleasant experience." Banes philosophized before chunking a chip shot that led to his third triple in a row.

"China Syndrome," Skully said looking at the hole in the ground left from Banes misfired wedge. "Meltdown is imminent."

Banes let out a scream and hurled his sand wedge into the air. WAPWAPWAPWAP went the club as it helicoptered its way into the pond behind the green.

"It's a good thing you can't see the scorecard, Banes, because then you'd be really pissed," Yaprickya said.

The group in front of them had just finished playing the 210-yard par three that lay ahead of Banes and decided to hang out and watch the fireworks.

"Twenty bucks says he puts it in the water," said the Vig.

"Another twenty dollars says the club follows," said Bimbo from his perch next to the green

Banes was last to hit, and his prospects didn't look good. Two out of the three players who hit before him had put their balls in the water. Banes couldn't even see the pin, and resigned himself to playing the hole with his eyes closed. The darkness had a calming effect and he actually put a good swing on his 5-wood that sent the ball arcing in a less than tragic trajectory toward the green. His eyes still closed, Banes listened for the telltale splash he half-expected to hear.

By the green, Bimbo yelled "incoming" and ducked while Vig just stared in amazement as Banes' ball took one hop on the green and then disappeared into the hole like the March Hare.

"YES!" Vig yelled while leaping off the ground like Michelson after winning the Masters.

The guys on the tee box also sprang to life.

"WOOOWOOOO!" Dick Yaprickya yelled. "YOUDAMAN BANES!"

"Is it on the green?" Banes asked, opening his eyes.

"YOU BLIND SQUIRREL, YOU," Skully gave his friend a bear hug. "YOU HOLED THE DAMN THING!"

"WHAT!?! BUT WAIT, I DIDN'T EVEN SEE IT! NOT AGAIN!"

With that, WAPWAPWAPWAP, Banes helicoptered his 5-wood into the pond to join his sand wedge.

"Ace Ventura, golf defective," said Vinny as he unscrewed the cap on his flask. "Congratulations."

Banes drank down the shot of single malt and as the elixir warmed his insides, he warmed to the realization that he'd just shot a hole-in-one. With his eyes closed.

"I'll never figure this game out," he confessed.

"I'll drink to that," said Skully, breaking out the first Schwing of the day and offering a bottle to each of the golfers.

As he raised his bottle, Banes waxed philosophic. "You know, what else can take a man from meltdown to euphoria in a matter of moments? Not beer, not heroin, not even a woman. Only one thing: Golf."

He was grinning so wide, he couldn't help but spill beer out the sides of his mouth and down the front of his shirt as he drank to the elusive game. Combined with the splotch of blood on his shorts that was by now the size of a grapefruit, Banes was a sight to behold as he took honors on the next tee and effortlessly drove the ball 290 yards splitting the center of the fairway.

"Nothing to this game."

That evening Banes paid for his euphoria dearly. While the sixteen of them were having dinner at Frank's, one by one they got up to get a drink. It was like a tag team. When one came back with his drink, the next would go. And as the recipient of a hole-in-one that he never got to see, the drinks were on Mr. Magoo.

He also found himself buying drinks for a couple at the bar whom he'd struck up a conversation with while waiting for the bartender to tally the bill. Witnessing his friends' constant parade to refresh their drinks, the woman said in a Southern drawl, "Why Chester, those friends of yours sure know how to knock 'em back."

"I'm painfully aware of that," Banes said looking at the bar bill.

When he got back to the table, the waitress was asking the rowdy crew if there was anything else she could get them.

Skully, who was feeling no pain, replied, "You, spread-eagled on the table."

Without hesitation she bent down shoving her cleavage in Skully's face and whispered loud enough for all to hear, "On my back or on my front?"

That sent the room up for grabs and Skully the half-millionaire took the check from her and said, "This one's on me boys."

From the restaurant they trekked up to The Pink Pony where they could gaze at more cleavage and punish Banes further for his ace by downing enough drinks to fill the water hazard that contained his sand wedge and 5-wood.

By midnight, nobody was feeling any pain, except for Banes when he sat down.

"Damn, I think I've got a shard of glass embedded in my ass from when I sat on my glasses today," he announced to the table.

"I've got just the thing," Skully said before

disappearing for a few minutes. He reappeared with one of the strippers decked out in a nurse's uniform.

"Guys, Nurse Naomi. Nurse Naomi, the Brawlers. And this here," he said pointing to Banes, "is your injured patient, Mr. Magoo, who sat on his glasses earlier today. Maybe you could take him to the ER and operate on his sorry ass."

"Why hello Mr. Magoo. Come right this way, the doctor will see you now." With that Nurse Naomi led Banes into the VIP room.

"Hurts so good," Obcorb said shaking his head.

"I'd like her to nurse my hangover tomorrow," Yaprickya said.

It wasn't ten minutes before Banes came back to the table holding his neck.

"She's not a nurse, she's a vampire. She bit me! Look!" Banes took his hand off his neck, revealing a big hickey. "Can you see anything?"

"Only that birthmark on your neck," the Vig said.

"Shite! What'll I tell Gwen?"

"Don't worry, it'll be gone by Sunday," Skully reassured him.

"Yeah, by Easter Sunday," Yaprickya said setting off a chain of laughter.

Obcorb began to sing a little ditty to the tune of "The Mickey Mouse Club."

"*H-I-C, K-E-Y, H-O-U-S-E*"

"*HICKEY HOUSE,*" everyone joined in, "*HICKEY HOUSE.*"

Skully finished the verse "*FOREVER LET US HOLD OUR RED NECKS HIGH.*"

"That's it," the Vig said. "You can tell Gwen you missed putting sunscreen on that spot."

Banes just groaned.

"I know," Yaprickya said, "You can tell her you were bouncing a ball on your wedge like Tiger, and whacked the ball into your neck."

"Hey, that's not bad," said Vinny, "It is about the size of a golf ball."

"*HICKEY HOUSE, HICKEY HOUSE*," they started up again.

"*HOW'M I GONNA LOOK HER IN THE EYE?*" Banes improvised.

For the next hour, they sounded like a broken record, going around the room with each of the guys improvising a punch line. And The Pink Pony would forevermore be known as The Hickey House among the Fall Brawlers.

The following morning, Vinny applied sunscreen liberally to Banes' hickey. "Now you just have to get some more collah on the rest of yah neck."

They were at a dog track which paled in comparison to Caledonia and The Dunes. The morning round was uneventful except for an incident on a green the course was having a hard time growing grass on. Bimbo was on in two strokes on number ten with a twelve-footer for birdie.

"Finally, a chance to put some points on my card," he said to the Vig, keeper of all bets.

As he put a smooth stroke on the ball, it hit one pothole after another and didn't come close to the hole.

"What the hell was that?" Bimbo said getting a little hot under the collar. "This isn't a putting surface, it's a bombed out war zone." When it took him three more putts to get his ball in the cup, he raised his putter in anger and yelled, "FIRE IN THE HOLE!" bringing the club down fiercely into the checkered turf surrounding the cup. He managed to excavate a chunk of soil far bigger than the cup itself.

"Well that should make it easier for the guys behind us to hole their putts," said the Vig as he attempted to replace the remnants of that hollowed ground.

While this was going on, the beverage cart arrived behind the green and as Bimbo was sulking back to his cart the girl looked over at the Vig and said, "Thanks for working on the green, I know we're having trouble with it."

"Oh, no problem," said Bimbo eyeing her golden locks.

"How about a couple of beers for the effort?" she said and comped the foursome a round.

"What are you doing this evening?" Bimbo wanted to know.

As they drove off, the Vig couldn't help but observe, "Only Bimbo could wreak havoc on a green like that and walk away with free beers for the effort. And a date, to boot."

The afternoon round found them on another course that shouldn't have found itself on their itinerary. Not only was it less than spectacular, the pace of play on Saturday afternoon was glacial.

So to kill time while waiting to hit their second shots on a roadside hole, Skully and Yaprickya chipped balls at the large neon sign bearing the name of the course.

"Twenty for the first to hit it," Yaprickya said.

It didn't take Skully more than one well-aimed shot. A neon tube exploded like a gunshot. "Woops. Pay up."

"Not so fast. I get a shot at it, too." With that, Yaprickya hit one over the sign and into the highway.

"Wow, look at that go," Skully said. "That car better watch out."

The sounds of tires screeching to a halt hid the sounds of Skully and Yaprickya laughing maniacally as they hightailed it back to the fairway where they acted as if nothing had happened.

"Maybe they'll blame it on Bimbo's group behind us," Yaprickya prayed.

Later that night they drove by to see if Skully's shot had affected the neon. Sure enough, instead of "Gray Rock" the sign now emblazoned the evening sky with the words "Gay Rock."

"Rock on, my light-in-the-FootJoys twenty smackers richer brother," said Yaprickya passing Skully a Jackson.

The only other casualty on the links that day was Banes, who was constantly nipping at his flask of Glenlivet and cursing "Nurse Dracula." His rationale was that if he got enough sauce in him, he'd burn more under the South Carolina sun, which would help disguise the hickey lathered in sunscreen.

But it didn't help his golf swing, or his memory. By the last nine of the day, he was constantly needing help recounting his score on any particular hole. As they were recounting the rounds and the bets that evening by the leader board, Obcorb aptly summed up Banes' condition in one word: "Glenesia." Brought on by too much Glenlivet.

"That sounds serious," said Skully. "I think we ought to take him back to see the Nurse."

"I'm not sure he wants to remember those rounds today," the Vig said. "Banes, you're still at the bottom of the leader board. Skully, on the other hand, made a big move today and is neck and neck with Obcorb going into the final round tomorrow."

"Speaking of necks, how is it, Banes?" Vinny asked.

"Don't ask. My neck got sunburned, but the hickey's still there, surrounded by a white outline because you dabbed too much sunscreen around it."

"Nevah could paint within the lines. It's actually rathah striking. Got kind of a bullseye look to it now."

"You know, I may have had Glenesia today, but I

didn't have Gwenesia. Couldn't stop thinking about what your sister is going to say when she sees it."

"I've got one word for you brothah-in-law: turtlenecks."

After grabbing a quick bite, they retreated to the beach to finish off the remaining cases of Schwing. Before leaving the restaurant, Bimbo recruited a table full of women to join them.

"Strictly market research," he said.

"Yeah, knowing you, Dr. Kinsey, you'll be researching their sex lives before the night is through," Skully said tossing him a beer.

Lucky for Banes, one of the girls who came back to the beach actually was a nurse, and helped him out by using a Q-tip to swab some self-tanning lotion on the white ring surrounding the hickey.

"At least it won't stand out as much now," she said.

"Thanks. How do you like the beer?"

"Schwingin', baby," she said, sounding a bit like Austin Powers. "Did Mike Myers make this? Isn't that what he and Dana Carvey used to say in Wayne's World? SCHWING!"

"Yes, they used to say that, but no, he didn't make the beer. See, Skully and I were playing golf one day, and passing the flask full of what we call "Swing Lube." Only we'd passed it one too many times and it came out "Schwing Lube." And when we went looking for a name for Skully's homebrew, we shortened it to Schwing. Make sense?"

"Your logic is flawless Spock. You know, I don't care what you call it when it tastes this good," she said, handing Banes her empty. "Can I have a refill?"

Banes handed her another.

"What I like about the name," she continued, "is it's got spirit. Or should I say 'schpirit?' I like its attitude."

"It's altitude isn't bad either," Bimbo cut in. "C'mon, it's time to limbo."

The sounds of reggae music filled the air as the crew spent the next hour trying to limbo under a piece of driftwood Bimbo propped up on the empty Schwing cases.

The following day, Skully and Obcorb battled it out on the front nine, but the pressure was too much for either of them, and soon bogies were followed by doubles and triples.

Out of nowhere, Banes made a quiet charge compiling a scorecard of pars, birdies and even a lone eagle that catapulted him into contention. He had given up any hope of winning The Fall Brawl, and that was his salvation. He shot a 77, the best round of his life, and when he walked into the clubhouse afterward, there was dead silence.

"What's wrong?" he asked. "Somebody die?"

"Yes," said the Vig. "Your buddies Skully and Obcorb both faded away, and don't ask me how, but someone came from behind and stole The Cup from them."

"You're kidding. Who?"

"You." The room exploded with hoots, applause and catcalls as the Vig handed Banes The Cup. "Perhaps we should call this The Schwing Cup from now on."

"Well, in that case." Banes took the last remaining six-pack of Schwing and emptied the contents into the huge cup. "I now christen thee The Schwing Cup."

"Or The Hickey Cup," said Yaprickya.

"*H-I-C*," Obcorb began to sing and soon the whole gang was caught up in another mind-numbing, ear-splitting rendition of "Hickey House" as they passed the cup around. Walt Disney rolled over in his grave, covering his ears.

On the drive back to Virginia—Schwing Cup seat belted into the backseat—the rain began to pelt the windshield and Skully began to snore in the passenger seat. A couple hours into the drive, he awoke and looked over at Banes behind the wheel. There was the hickey, still looming large, though not quite as noticeable as the day before. And there was Banes, still grinning from ear to ear from his win, his best round ever, and his first hole-in-one. Only one thing was missing.

"Uh, Banes, where are your glasses?"

"Sat on them, remember?"

"So how can you see the road without 'em?"

"Hell, with all this rain, I couldn't see the road with 'em."

"I'M BEING CHAUFERRED BY MR. MAGLOO!" Skully screamed to no one.

Skully made Banes pull over so that he could take the helm and as they did their Chinese fire drill in the rain, he noticed a splotch of red on the front seat. "By the way, your ass is bleeding again, Magoo." Skully wiped the blood off with his sleeve before sitting down.

But Banes was already drifting off into dreamland where he could replay the high points of the weekend.

When he got home that evening, Gwen immediately spotted the mark on his neck and asked, "What happened, you get hit by a golf ball?"

"How'd you know?" Banes asked, relieved.

"Isn't it obvious? Here, let me give it a kiss," she said softly pecking at his neck.

"When you're done there, I've got another boo-boo down here," he said pointing to the bloodstain on the back of his pants.

Nothing like walking in from a wild weekend with the boys and asking your wife to kiss your bleeding ass.

Gwen bent over feigning a kiss and opted instead to give him a good spank.

"OW!" Through the pain Banes realized that the nurse must have missed a shard of glass. "What'd you do that for?"

"That's for all your shenanigans I'll never know about," Gwen said. "Now let's get the Betadine and clean up that bloody butt of yours."

As he dropped his drawers, Banes said, "You'd have made a fine nurse, Gwen."

YOU GOLF GIRL

The morning after The Fall Brawl, Banes woke to the sound of the doorbell ringing and the regrettable taste of three days and nights of hangin' with the old buds in his mouth.

"Can you get that, hon?" Gwen called from the bathroom.

"Ugh," Banes said with all of the eloquence of a bear being roused from his mid-winter hibernation.

He stumbled down the stairs wiping the sleep from his eyes and flung open the door. There stood Skully's girlfriend Barb decked out in a sexy little golf outfit.

"Good morning, Chet. Happy to see me?" Barb's eyes drifted south to a small pup tent in Banes' pajamas.

Banes' eyes followed hers and he turned a shade of crimson.

"Oh, sorry Barb," he said. "Just woke up."

"Well you better get moving soldier, we tee off in ten minutes."

"Huh? But it's Monday, isn't it? The club's closed."

"Not this Monday. It's Columbus Day. Time to discover that your bride and I are challenging you two worthless golf bums to a match."

"You're kidding, right?"

"Would I kid a guy who's standing ten hut in his boxers with only nine minutes to get his sorry der-riere to the first tee where his wife and I are going to take him and his buddy Skully to the cleaners? Would I do that to you, Chester?"

Over Barb's shoulder, Banes could see Skully sitting behind the wheel of his Jeep. He gave his friend a salute.

"Well I'll be an onkey's muncle."

"See you down there."

Banes ascended the stairs to his bedroom where Gwen emerged wearing a plaid green skirt and a pink polo shirt.

"How come you didn't tell me about this?" he asked his wife.

"Surprise." She pecked his cheek and whispered in his ear, "Whatsamatta sailor, don't you wanna play a round?"

The pup tent reappeared and Banes pulled her closer.

"Uh, uh. No time for that." Gwen broke free and bounded down the stairs. "Get your ass in gear. We tee off in five."

Banes grabbed a two-minute shower with an icy

finish and did a quick search for some clean golf clothes but all he could find was a pair of patch madras pants and a yellow shirt.

"Hello, Chester," he said to his rode-hard-put-away-wet reflection in the bathroom mirror and hightailed it out to the car where Gwen was waiting.

"My, aren't we sporty today?" she said raising an eyebrow at his outfit.

"Hello, Dolly," Banes said through pierced lips as he kissed her on the cheek.

"Ouch. You're prickly."

"Sorry, no time to shave."

It was a close shave making their tee time. Banes found his friend Skully, also unshaven, and Barb on the first tee.

"You're early," Skully said.

"And the early worm catches the birdie," Banes said. "I feel sorry for the girls. We've just come off a 108-hole warm-up weekend. They don't stand a chance."

"Put your greenery where your pie hole is, Tiger. These two pussycats are going to show you who's got a game," Gwen said pulling a tee from behind her ear.

"You tell 'em, Gwen," said Barb. "We're gonna show 'em who owns the holes."

"Boy, you two can sure talk some trash," said Skully. "Dollar skins?"

"Make it two, big spender," Gwen challenged and tossed a tee in the air that pointed to Skully when it landed. "Show us how it's undone, Skully."

"You asked for it Gwen. We'll give you each a stroke a hole."

"Very generous," she said. "But schtupid."

"Banes why don't you take us out," Skully said.

"My honor, your honor?" Banes walked to the

blue markers and stuck a tee in the ground. "He offered his honor."

"And she honored his offer," Skully picked up on his friends train of thought.

"And all night long he was on her and off her, yeah, yeah, we've heard it before," Gwen completed the ditty adding her own commentary. "Are you two ever going to tee off or are we going to have to cite you for terrapin play? Maybe I'll start calling you Chester Sabbatini."

"So you want to tango, do you," Banes said addressing the ball and taking his driver slowly back back back back until he reached parallel where he made the ill-advised move of taking the club back another six inches before initiating a ferocious downswing and sending a big slice off to the right.

"Nice banana," Barb said. "Is that what you were hiding in your shorts when you answered the door this morning, Chet?"

"I guess I'm just a little stiff," Banes said.

"Little being the operative word," Gwen added.

"Now, now, cut him some slack," said Skully. "He is on the fairway."

"Yeah, the fairway for number ten. Why don't you put one right next to his?" Gwen suggested.

But Skully didn't take her advice. He started the ball out right down the center but put a good draw on it and the ball sailed over the left bunker and hit the cart path which sent it bounding out of bounds.

"Overcooked it," Banes said. "Make the next one al dente, will ya?"

Skully re-teed and hit a similar shot with a little less juice which found a home in the fairway bunker.

"Golf's a beach," said Barb as she and Gwen drove down the cart path to the red tees.

"Not the only beach out here," Skully said under his breath to Banes.

Barb teed off first and bisected the fairway. Gwen followed suit landing within ten yards of her.

"Beginner's luck," Banes called out to them.

"It's all downhill from here," Skully added.

Gwen and Barb beamed as they got back in their cart. They easily won the hole, and the boys were so unglued from losing the 1st hole, they proceeded to tank the 2nd as well. By the 3rd hole they partially righted their ship and tied the girls' bogie with a par. As they stepped to the 4th tees, Skully and Banes were confident a momentum shift was imminent, and told Barb and Gwen that they were pressing the bet.

"Is that like the doubling cube in backgammon?" Barb asked.

"Sort of," said Skully.

"Well why don't we just use one of those?" Gwen asked pulling a doubling cube from her bag. Before the boys could raise an eyebrow she handed them the die with the number four facing up and said "We'll double you back."

"Let's see, that makes this hole with four times two…eight buckaroos," said Banes.

"Sixteen," Gwen corrected him. "We are doing carryovers, aren't we?"

"I stand corrected, my dear. Sixteen. Schweet sixteen."

"Schweet!" Skully sounded like a bullfrog. "Schweet. Schweet."

The boys took the box first, since the red tees were down the hill in front of them. The 4th at River Creek is a 511-yard par five with a 230-yard carry over a pond if you want to bite off all you can chew. The safer play was to fire one over the middle of the pond to the fairway beyond, but Banes was never one to play it safe. He aimed between the fountain in the center of the pond and the willow tree on the far bank, and put what he thought was a good swing on the ball, but it started tailing right and kept fading until it dove right of the willow and into the hazard.

"Damn!" he pounded the head of his driver into the tee box.

"There's that banana again," Barb teased.

"C'mon Skully," Banes said to his partner. "Put one out there."

"Coming right up," Skully said. "But first…" He reached into the cart and grabbed the doubling cube turning it to eight. "We'll double."

"You're on," said Barb. "That makes this drive worth thirty-two dollars. No pressure."

Skully swaggered up to the tee and lined up to hit it right over the fountain. He took a nice smooth backswing, but as his club made its way toward his Hogan 3 Apex Tour, he could hear the pressure cooker inside begin to whistle and he overcooked another drive sending it hooking beyond the fairway and into the cart path again where it took a huge hop and landed who knows where.

"Wow, Skully, that could be on the other side of the street," Barb said reassuringly.

Skully just shook his head, slammed his driver back in his bag and got in the cart.

Once again, the girls took full advantage of the situation putting two in the fairway, reaching the green in regulation and both two-putting for their pars.

"Well, that was a waste," said Gwen.

"Whaddya mean? You just won thirty-two dollars!" said Banes.

"Yeah, but we didn't need our stroke to do it," she smiled fondling the doubling cube. "Why don't we give you a chance to win your money back?" She handed Banes the cube with the number sixteen facing up.

"Thank you dear, but you can only press when you're down."

"Oh, this isn't a press honey, this is the doubling cube. If you've got it, you can use it."

"We'll accept," Skully stepped in and took the cube. "Sixteen times two. This hole's worth another thirty-two dollars. Redemption is at hand."

"And temptation just out of reach," said Barb as she put her palm flat on the ground doing a yoga stretch.

Skully and Banes couldn't help but stare at her lithe body.

"Snap out of it and hit the ball," Gwen said.

Banes rose to the occasion and put one on the green of the par three 5th. Skully then did the same, getting inside of Banes.

"Hey, you Rocked me!" Banes said.

"You Rocked me?" Barb asked.

"Yeah, he got inside me. Like Rock Hudson."

"You guys are gross," she said and proceeded to Rock Skully by putting her tee shot inside of his.

"You Rock, partner," said Gwen as she reached her fist out to Barb. Gwen then sailed her ball onto the green as well.

"Something's wrong with this picture," said Banes. "When did you two become Annika and Michelle?"

"You know all those weekends when you guys deserted us to play golf with each other?"

"Uh, yeah."

"We've been taking lessons and practicing."

"Hey, no fair!"

"All's fair in love and war," Gwen said to Banes. "And this, my dear, is war."

"More like Armageddon," said Barb.

"Looks like they're taking no prisoners," said Skully. "Let's go sink a putt."

"Or wave a white flag," said Banes grabbing a white towel out of the cart and twirling it above his head.

He and Gwen missed their birdie putts and both tapped in for par, which left Skully up next. As he lined up his putt, he noticed Barb right behind him.

"Watcha doin'?" he asked.

"Going to school on you."

"Well let me teach you a thing or two." Skully put a smooth strike on his putt and the ball found the back of the cup for a birdie.

"Yeah, Baby!" Banes high-fived his partner.

Barb put her ball down and picked up her ball marker. She took a practice swing while standing behind her ball looking at the cup, and then got up and hit her putt. Like Skully's, it was tracking, but Barb's died on the lip of the cup.

"How does that not go in?" Gwen asked.

"It's sitting on a lip the size of Angelina Jolie's," Skully said, reaching for the pin.

Just as he picked up the stick, the ball took

another half turn in slow motion and found the bottom of the cup with a resounding "PLUNK."

Banes stood by the cart waving the white towel.

"No blood," Skully said walking to the cart.

"Skully, my love," said Barb. "I believe we were stroking there, which, if I'm not mistaken, would give us the hole, would it not?"

"Stroke this," Skully said with his putter between his legs.

"That's another $32, boys," Gwen said marking the scorecard.

Banes continued waving the towel as he got back in the cart.

The boys were shell-shocked as the girls went on to win the next three holes.

"Who are these guys?" Skully said to Banes and the two of them drove up to the 9th tee feeling like Butch and Sundance being relentlessly pursued by a posse.

"Maybe it's time to put the pedal to the metal," Banes said picking up the doubling cube.

"Go for it," said Skully.

"What have we here?" asked Gwen as Banes presented her with the cube bearing the number thirty-two.

"A token of my love for you dear," answered Banes.

As she turned the cube to sixty-four and handed it back to her husband, Gwen sang, *"Will you still need me, will you still feed me, when I'm sixty-four?"*

"They're not only out-golfing us," Skully said. "They're out-attituding us to boot. Let's rally!"

He and Banes summoned their golf reserves and found the fairway from the tee of the long par five along the river.

But the girls were unflappable, and made their own drives onto the fairway look like a walk in the park.

"You know, Gwen," Barb said leaving the tee box, "I could grow to like this game."

By the time they reached the green, it was a putt off between Gwen, who was lying four, and Banes, who was lying three, to determine who would win the hole. Gwen was away with Banes a foot inside her.

As she bent down to mark her ball, Banes positioned himself behind her.

"What are you doing?" she asked.

"Going to school on you."

"Do you always pay that much attention to a schoolgirl?" she asked and began polishing her ball with her skirt. In doing so, she revealed she wasn't wearing any underwear. Banes couldn't help but notice, and the next thing he knew, the pup tent reappeared.

Gwen sank her putt.

He had to do the same, or they'd be down nine skins to the girls. At $128-a-pop.

165

But as he was lining up his putt, Gwen bent over to retrieve her ball from the cup and flashed him a moon.

Banes stood at attention and tried to putt but it was hopeless. He pulled it left of the cup.

"Looks like you yanked it," said Gwen.

"Or need to," said Barb.

"Now that's hitting below the belt," Skully came to his friend's defense.

"Let's see," Gwen said looking at the card, "Sixty-four times nine times two dollars. Anyone got a calculator?"

"I gotta hit the ATM," Skully said.

"I could use a cold shower," said Banes.

"What about the back nine?" asked Barb.

Skully and Banes both grabbed towels from the cart and began waving them in the air.

"We surrender."

When they got back home, Banes took a long

cold shower and then Gwen hit him with the cold hard facts.

"You owe me $1152, Chester."

"What!?!"

"Sixty-four times nine times two dollars. That's 1,152 clams."

"Yikes. Here's a first installment." He handed her a couple of singles.

"Two bucks?"

"I'm a little short of cash."

"So how do you plan on settling the bet, big boy?" She uncrossed and crossed her legs doing her best Sharon Stone imitation from *Basic Instinct*.

"How 'bout I'll be your love slave for a day?" He raised an eyebrow, but Gwen just shook her head. He decided to sweeten the offer. "A week? A month? A year?"

"I've got a better idea," she said. "How about you give up golf for a year?"

"Oh come on Gwen, why would I want to do that?"

"I can think of 1150 reasons why."

"I'd really prefer to be your slave, master."

"And I'd prefer not to be a golf widow."

"Now, now. I don't play that often."

"Often enough for me to take up golf in your absence and then beat you at your own game."

"How humiliating is that? You'd think that would be payment enough."

"Nice try Chester. Admit it. You're a golfoholic."

"Okay, I admit it. Are we square now?"

"Not so fast. You've got to get some therapy. See if you can overcome your addiction."

"Addiction? The only thing I'm addicted to is your love." With that, he sidled up to her and kissed her on the neck.

"Spoken like a true addict. Seriously Chet, you need some help."

"And where am I going to find that? Dr. Phil? Dr. Melfi?"

"Try this." She handed him an ad she'd clipped out of the local paper.

"Golfoholics Anonymous? You're kidding, right?"

"It's either that or $1150. Your choice."

"You sure you won't reconsider the love slave option."

"Oh I don't think I have to pay for that," she said bounding up the stairs and flashing him another moon in the process.

Banes took the stairs two at a time in hot pursuit.

GOLFOHOLICS ANONYMOUS

Banes walked up to the podium and greeted the crowd.

"Hi, my name is Chester, and I'm a golfoholic."

"HI CHESTER!" they said back in unison.

"I guess it all began back in '84 when my girl-friend Gwen, who's now my lovely wife, whispered in my ear, 'Do you wanna play a round?' and then mistook the animal desire in my eye and the drool emanating from my lips as a passion for the game. The game of golf, that is.

"So we played. And it was tolerable. And we

played. And it was almost enjoyable. And we played, and we played, and we played. And it was almost better than sex. And that was pretty damn good.

"Until I started tearing up the greens more often than we were rolling in the hay. That's when I knew I might have a problem. But it was our wedding day when everything really started to unravel. All because of my golf Jones.

"Of course my judgment was impaired as a result of a few too many toasts at the rehearsal dinner the night before. But the old gang was in town, and each of them had something to say. And each time, I raised my glass in return. A big Dom Perignono.

"May 1st, our wedding day, came way too soon when three of my old buddies appeared at my bed-side with clubs in hand. An alarmed voice inside me cried 'Mayday! Mayday!'

"I recall one of my groom goons, Dick Yaprickya, saying, 'C'mon, Banes, day's a wasting.'

"'But I'm a wasted,' I moaned, wrapping my head in my pillow.

"'Here, take a couple of these and you'll be fine,' Obcorb said as he tried to shove a couple of Titleists in my mouth.

"My best man Skully cut to the chase. 'Just get your lazy soon-to-be-hitched ass out of bed and get with the program, Banes, I gave up my virginity for this tee time.'

"A tee time wasn't the only thing he had persuaded the beautiful Beth, who worked in our local pro shop, to give us. Bethpage Beth, we called her. She had made an appearance at my bachelor party the week before, thanks to Skully's persuasive skills. But I digress.

"So I dragged my butt out of bed and off we went to the Black Course and played a therapeutic round, finishing just before the rain came down. We played in black tie since we had no time to change in between the golf and the wedding. Our tee time was at ten and the wedding began at three. That didn't leave a lot of time for the 19th hole, let alone a change of clothes.

"And it wasn't until the 19th hole that Skully realized something was missing. Something that had been in his care and possession until very recently. The wedding band.

"'When was the last time I used it?' he asked us.

"'Used it?' There was a look of bewilderment on our collective faces.

"'Yeah, as a ball marker,' he replied, stating what he believed to be the obvious. 'I think it was on the 17th.'

"'You're kidding, right?' I said looking at him like a deer in the headlamps.

"'Maybe it's an omen,' he said with a raised eyebrow. 'You sure you want to go through with this, Banes? Getting married can put a damper on your golf game, you know.'

"'Dammit, Skully, we've got to find that ring!' I implored. I was no longer Chester Banes, I was Frodo.

"'To the ring!' Skully raised his glass, and we all drained our drinks before going out to scour Middle Earth for the missing band of gold. In our tuxes. In the rain, which had gone from a threat to a torrent since we'd finished our round.

"We worked our way from the clubhouse to the 18th green, and from the green to the tee box. An hour passed, and a small ocean fell from the sky. We were lost ships on a green sea, and I was feeling more than a little green around the gills.

"Just when I thought I was going to lose either my lunch or my mind, I heard Skully shout the two most welcome words my ears could possibly hear, 'Got it!'

"'It was right where I thought it would be,' he

said proudly, holding the ring up for all to see. 'On the 18th tee box.'

"'So why didn't we check there first?' I wondered aimlessly.

"'The glass is always half empty, isn't it Banes?' Skully said, putting his arm around me. 'Look on the bright side, will ya? We've got the ring.'

"'Yeah, and the wedding doesn't start for another, oh, ten minutes,' Obcorb added.

"'Too bad the church is a twenty-minute drive on a good day,' Yaprickya rained on our already drenched parade.

"So we all piled into Skully's '68 Camaro convertible and set a new land-speed record between Bethpage Black and the little white church Gwen and I were to marry in. But on the way, a cop wielding a radar gun took issue with our speed and pulled us over.

"'Late for your own funeral?' he asked.

"'Wedding,' Skully replied and pointed at me. 'His. But it might as well be his funeral if we don't get there in the next five minutes.'

"He could have written us up. Hell, he could have locked us up and thrown away the key if he'd wanted. Instead he simply said, 'Follow me,' and sped off in his car, lights flashing and siren wailing.

"We pulled up to the chapel in no time, less than ten minutes late. Feeling greatly relieved, my groomsmen and I walked down the aisle of the full church grinning from ear to ear. Until we noticed the horrified looks we were getting from the wedding guests. And the occasional laugh, snicker, snoot, howl and cry from friends doubled over in the pews.

"In our wet, wrinkled tuxes, we must have looked like something *The Cat in the Hat* dragged in.

"And the most horrified look came from Gwen, my beautiful bride to be, when she walked down the aisle moments later only to discover a wilted penguin at the altar.

"'What happened to you?' she asked.

"I averted my eyes and looked down at my shoes. Gwen's eyes followed.

"'Aren't those your golf shoes?' she inquired, somewhat mystified, until a knowing look came over her.

"'Only black pair I own,' I lied.

"My name is Chester, and I'm a golfoholic," Banes concluded, stepping away from the podium.

The crowd applauded. Al wiped a tear from his eye. "Weddings always make me cry," he confessed.

"They make me want to play golf," Fred shot back at him.

"Well, let's get a move on guys, we'll be late for our tee time," Skully rallied the troops.

With that Skully, Banes, Fred and Al ended the

debut meeting of the River Creek Chapter of Golfoholics Anonymous and walked out of the clubhouse to the first tee.

"You know, I have to admit this G.A. stuff was one of your wife's better ideas," Skully said, patting his pal Banes on the back.

"To Gwen!" Banes raised his flask before unleashing 270 yards of pure passion.